THE SEVEN SOULS
OF
ROLDIN BENIRUS

BOOK ONE
LEGEND OF THE MARKED MAN

RANSOM PRESTRIDGE

K&L Publishing
822 N 9th Street
St. Joseph, MO 64501

Visit our website at www.klpub.com

ISBN-10: 0991139356
ISBN-13: 978-0991139354

Printed in the United States of America

First Edition: August 2016

10 9 8 7 6 5 4 3 2 1

For all you loners out there.
May you learn to slay your own demons.

and

For my mother, for showing me what real strength is,
and for always letting me walk my own path.

TABLE OF CONTENTS

PROLOGUE
TOO MUCH COIN

Roldin yawned long and wide, covering his mouth with the back of his sleeve. For an instant the young boy's vision blurred and the constantly moving world before him vanished in a haze before it returned, dreary and rainy as it always was. The muddy road stretched out before him with a depressing sameness, kissed by farms and wooden fences on either side. The ruts the cart's wheels made in the mud were deep and jagged, marking where he had come from, which looked very similar to where he was going.

His sleeve smelled faintly of blueberries, reminding him of how hungry he was, and his stomach groaned in abrupt protest. His nose also itched. The rain pelted him mercilessly and soaked him through his tattered cloak. There was no one position that was more comfortable than the next; pain found him no matter how he sat. The wheel hit a rock and jostled him. His shoulder bumped up against a barrel next to him in the crowded cart, aggravating an already sore part of his arm where it had been hit many times before. The boy shifted with a stifled whimper. He turned to face the road ahead.

He spotted the back of his father's head. The man's long, greasy, dark hair was turning grey at the temples, he noticed, and thinner on top. His father was thinner, too. Both of them were, as business and food had been scarce.

Roldin forgot the name of the county they were passing

1

through. It looked as poor and dreary as the last, and didn't impress him much. Bored, the boy felt like calling out to his father, maybe asking him to tell stories of his time on a merchant ship where he'd "traveled 'round the world." But, sullenly, he thought better of it. The flask that sat next to his father already rattled hollowly. The sun was barely in the middle of the sky, a dull candle fighting to break through grey clouds, and his father's ill temper radiated from him like a foul stench. When he was in these moods, Roldin knew, it was best to stay quiet.

The cart stopped. His father started talking to two farmers passing in the opposite direction, trying to sell them grain. As mean as he was, his father knew how to sweet-talk. The smile he was capable of giving to those he tried to work his peddler magic on – yellowed-teeth and all – could put anyone at ease. The two farmers chatted with him for a time, talking of the weather and a brewing war between this county and a neighboring rival. The tensions were making trade hard, and they feared for their harvest. War was never good for crops. Eventually, they made some excuse and went on their way. Roldin winced as his father's gaze followed them and his cheery smile directly melted into a scowl at the back of their heads. He caught his son looking at him and the scowl deepened. Roldin spun around quickly and stared out the back of the cart as it lurched forward. The two of them continued in silence. Roldin watched the two farmers walk off down the road, wide hats barely keeping off the rain, until they vanished from view. Then the road was empty again.

Roldin pulled his knees up close and hugged them. When the monotony became too much for him, he reached across the cart to his small satchel and brought out his favorite – and, currently, only – book. The cover was well-worn and ragged and the deep embossing on the spine, just barely legible, read "The Pauper Prince and the Sword of Kuralee." The engraved lettering felt familiar under his fingers. The boy arranged himself carefully and pulled his cloak further over his head to shelter the pages as he turned them, not really reading them – he knew the story by heart – just experiencing them. It was a story about a boy, much like him, who was a young pauper who, one day, found a magic sword. He grew powerful and strong, and with the sword he saved a princess from bad men, then he fought for a king, saving a kingdom from an army of demons, and was made a prince. He married the princess, and they lived happily ever after.

The cart stopped again and Roldin looked up to see a family of travelers, in a cart of their own, stop on the opposite side of the road. There were a couple of men, a woman, and a little girl sitting there. His father transformed into the consummate peddler, striking up a conversation with one of the men as he turned around and began showing off his goods, taking out the best ones first. Roldin registered that his father didn't need his help so he returned to his book and drifted off into the pages.

His father's tone-of-voice shifted a little. Roldin immediately recognized the muted agitation. The traveler didn't show interest in anything he was offered, so his father started taking out the less flashy items, rummaging around in the cart a little more roughly than he had to. Roldin knew the best way to handle that mood was to be invisible, so he tried to make himself smaller.

"I'd be interested in that book," Roldin heard one the travelers say. He understood what that meant, but he tried to hide the book under himself anyway, only struggling a little when his father walked over to yank it out of his hands. Roldin was careful to keep his face under his cloak as he turned to see the peddler hand the book over and take a handful of coins. Roldin received no apologetic glance; no sad shrug. His father just climbed back on the cart and prompted the horses to continue.

Roldin hugged his knees again. Anger began to build up inside him, though he dared not show it. Then he saw the traveler hand the book to his little girl. She was younger than Roldin, maybe seven or eight, and grabbed it with youthful eagerness. It meant something to him, he suddenly realized, to pass on the happy story to someone else.

"You'll really like that book!" he called to the girl. She

looked up and smiled at him, and Roldin smiled in return. His father muttered at him to stop yelling. The boy sat back, watched the other cart vanish down the road, and wished the girl would get as much out of the book as he had. Besides, the story was in his head. Roldin closed his eyes and could see the words on the page as clearly as if it were in his hands, helping him forget the rain and the creaking cart wheels and his father's mood.

By early afternoon they came to the edge of a town. It was more than that, he saw with wonder, peering over his father's shoulder. It was a castle — Adren, the county seat. Stone spires reached high into the sky, seeming to touch the clouds, and there were more people in the town square of the hamlet that lay under its shadow than he had ever seen in one place in his entire life. Men and women and children came and went, carts or arms full of goods of one sort or another, looking to buy and to sell.

His father eyed them all with coins in his eyes and he instantly stopped the cart, commanding Roldin to get out and set up shop. The two arranged their finest goods up front, others in tiers toward the back in a carefully choreographed display. Roldin struggled to lift the one chest that was full to the brim with what his father called "shady things." This was always the chest where the boy would sit, so as not to attract attention to it.

His father once again transformed into the cheery peddler, taking on his easy smile and hocking his goods with a friendly voice that belied his drunkenness and hunger. Roldin joined in a higher-pitched version of his father's song-of-sales, but his heart wasn't in it. A few people stopped to look over their goods, and a couple even bought some things, but most ignored the two of them. There were better-looking carts, with prettier peddlers and cheaper goods, elsewhere in the town square.

They managed to trade a box full of silks for a few coins and a loaf of bread. Roldin's stomach ached looking at it, and it was only mostly gone by the time his father reluctantly handed it over. "I do most of the work, I get most of the food," was his father's most common adage. Roldin was used to it and happy to get what he could. He smiled and said, "We're doing good,

4

aren't we, Da? It's a good day; things are going to look up!" His father said nothing.

Three children ran up to the cart — followed more slowly by their mother — and looked over the displayed goods. One of the little girls picked up a doll that caught her eye. The child fawned over it while Roldin's father smiled indulgently but watched her like a hawk. Finally the mother asked how much he wanted for it and balked at the asking price. His father tried to comment on the doll's quality but the woman cut him off, naming a price of her own. The peddler laughed, though there was no mirth in it. When the mother wouldn't budge, he bent down, snatched the doll out of the girl's fingers, and threw it back into the cart, hard. Roldin could see the throw had broken it. The girl started crying as her mother led her and the other children away, glaring back at the both of them. The peddler's mood plummeted further.

Night fell. The rain finally stopped, leaving the world soaked and shimmering in the pale moonlight. Roldin was chilled to the bone but packed the cart without complaint and led the horses through the town to the cheapest inn they could find. While Roldin wiped down the horses, his father paid a few bored-looking guards extra to make sure nothing was taken from the cart overnight. Then, together, they went inside.

The common room was warm, dry, and inviting. A pair of minstrels played a flute and sang near the fire, and Roldin instantly felt a smile on his face. His father led him to a table near the back and planted them at a small booth much further away from the fire and song than Roldin would have liked. His father ordered several tumblers of whiskey and a single loaf of bread with butter. The boy attacked the bread ravenously while the peddler quickly drank himself into oblivion.

His father kept company only with the cup in his hand, so Roldin was alone with his thoughts again. He tried to listen to the scattered conversations around him as the many voices snaked their way through the tavern to his ears. Several patrons mentioned that the lord of this town was getting desperate for mercenaries and would do anything to overthrow his neighbor. Hushed comments were made about how ruthless the young Lord Twill was. Roldin also heard about a fair coming next month with dancers, and jugglers, and actors, and singers, and animals from far away. The boy turned to his father, intending to beg they stay until the fair arrived so they could see it, but found the peddler had his arms around a serving girl and was trying to get her into his lap. He was drunk, and she was not, and she landed a mighty slap on his face. Roldin winced.

His father flew into a rage. The man, skinny and hungry as he was, had a fierce strength in his bony hands, and he grabbed the woman with a snarl. Two men rushed to her defense and his father was quickly outnumbered. Roldin looked around in a panic. A man wearing the red tunic of a county guard leaned against the bar, watching the fight with little intention of intervening. The two men soon overpowered his father, knocked him to the ground and began kicking him mercilessly. They were laughing, the serving girl too, and a few of the other tavern patrons joined in, as if the whole thing were a comic performance.

"Curse you all!" his father snarled between kicks. "May the demons — "A hard kick from a drunken man took the wind right out of him. He gasped and choked. "May the demons take your hides!" Still laughing, the men wandered away, back to their cups and comrades.

Roldin bent down to help his father up but he was pushed away, roughly. Blood leaked from the peddler's temple and nose, and he was holding his ribs in an awkward way. He sat up, finally, then stood, finished his whiskey with a few gulps, and grabbed Roldin by the shoulder to lean on him up the stairs to their room. The boy tried to glare angrily at the guard as they passed. The man remained unmoving, just watching them quietly, almost thoughtfully. Roldin feared his fierce look appeared more worried than scary.

The boy had much practice treating his father's wounds and was a fair study with a needle and thread. This time the wounds weren't as bad as they'd looked downstairs, but they needed a good washing. Roldin did the best he could. His father would usually be yelling and cursing him by this time, and taking out on his son what he couldn't take out on other, larger men. Tonight, his father was different. He looked tired. Defeated. The boy got the bleeding to stop, bandaged him, and let his father lie back in bed.

He stood and leaned against the windowsill. There was nothing to see in the black, but he could hear the rain had started to fall again, in large drops, and he was glad they had found an inn tonight. Roldin was tired of sleeping on the ground, and he appreciated having a roof over his head for a change.

A knock at the door broke his grateful reverie. Before the boy could get up, his father was on his feet with a dagger gripped in the hand behind his back. It was master-forged steel — one of the most expensive things his father owned — and the surly man knew exactly how to use it when he had to. The peddler opened the door, slowly.

On the other side was the same county guard Roldin had seen in the common room. The guard's red tunic gleamed dully in the candlelight from the hallway. "I saw you tonight. Saw you today in the town square, too," the guard said with a casual drawl. "Not much business lately?"

"What do you want?" his father said. "Going to kick me while I'm down, like them others?"

The guard shook his head. "You're a peddler. A man of business. My lord wants to know if you would like to peddle something. Come with me," he said.

Roldin stood up, fists clenched. "You're not taking my da anywhere!" he screamed hoarsely. The last time his father had been taken away by a guard he'd been gone a week, rotting in a cell. Roldin had gone quite hungry that week and his father's mood had been worse than ever afterward. He had no wish to repeat that situation.

"My lord just wants to talk to him," the guard assured

Roldin with a warm smile. The boy thought it looked like the man had too many teeth. "I promise you," he said, turning back to Roldin's father, "there's quite a bit of coin involved. You'll be serving my lord and Adren, and they pay very well."

"No, you're lying, you're not taking him to some jail!" the boy shouted, and moved in front of his father.

The peddler pushed him back roughly and Roldin fell to the floor. "Shut up," he growled at his son. To the guard, "How much coin?"

"That is for my lord to decide," the guard said. "You must come with me, now, to find out."

His father told him to stay put, then left without another word. Roldin sat on the bed, alone, scared he would never see his father again. His father had done worse than try to grope a barmaid in the past and not been arrested then, so maybe this was a misunderstanding? As much as he feared his father's temper, the possibility of being alone terrified him more. He lit another candle against the dark and listened to the rain drum on the window.

As the night wore on, Roldin's fatigue caught up with him and he drifted in and out of sleep. Dreams came to him in unsettling bits and pieces. In one, he dreamed he was back in his cart, listening to the wheels turning, watching the road pass by endlessly. Instead of a road of dirt or mud, they were traveling on a path of stars — stars that barely kept the inky blackness behind them at bay. He turned to his father to ask what was wrong, but it was not his father driving the cart. A bloody skeleton held the reigns.

In another dream, an indistinguishable form in the darkness smiled mirthlessly at him and pricked his left hand with a knife, drawing blood. He stirred in his sleep and half woke. The rain had stopped again and the candles had burnt out but there was the slightest bit of moonlight streaming in through the window. Roldin's hand itched, and he thought he could see a small bit of dried blood on his palm. He wondered how he could have hurt it. He half-remembered the dream, but that didn't make any sense, it had not been real...and the thought left him as his mind again wandered through a disturbed dream world.

#

It was still dark when his father shook him roughly. "Get up, we're leaving," the peddler growled. Roldin's sudden relief that his father was back was tempered by the odd, pale quality of the man's face. It was more drawn than usual, and his eyes were bloodshot. As he wiped his brow, Roldin noticed he had a new bandage around his wrist, too.

"What happened?" the boy asked.

"Nothing," the peddler grumbled. Then he smiled slightly. "Got paid." He said no more after that.

He ushered Roldin quickly through the empty common room and out the back door to where the horses and cart were hitched, waiting. The boy kept scratching at his palm, where the blood had dried, sticky and achy, and he wondered again what had happened. His father goaded the horses to a speed that scared him. He looked furtively behind them, expecting to see pursuing guards, but found nothing. The streets of the city were as empty and quiet as a graveyard.

They left town by a different road than they had come in, into a heavy forest. The pre-dawn air was chilly and Roldin pulled his tattered cloak around himself as tightly as he could, the barrel next to him already chafing painfully against his arm. He was shaking more than he thought he should. He fretted with his palm again.

About a mile from the town walls his father pulled the cart to the side of the road and simply stopped. Roldin peered around in alarm — but saw no sign of any danger. His father leaned back in his seat, uncorked a bottle, and didn't even spare his confused son a glance. Soon, though, a figure on a horse rode out of the woods towards them. With a start, Roldin recognized the same guard from their earlier exchange, and behind him, two more guards with a smaller cart of their own. The only thing balanced on it was a single chest.

"You're late," the guard said. He gestured, and the other two guards dismounted and carried the chest over to the peddler's cart.

"Move," his father grumbled at him. Roldin barely had time to slip off the cart before the two soldiers placed the chest where he had been sitting.

The first guard turned to his father again. "As agreed," and put his hand out. His father took the hand and shook it. The guard said, "There will only be one, for now. It was a hard battle. The others will collect in time."

Roldin had no idea what that meant. Surely the tavern brawl couldn't have yielded anything worth keeping in a chest? The guard shot the boy a quick look, and the three men in red rode off back towards the city at an unusually hasty gallop, their empty cart clattering loudly behind them.

His father said nothing. The boy was not sure what to do. Roldin stood there, in the middle of the road, behind the cart, his cloak hugging his shoulders. His shivering worsened. He eyed the cart, especially where the chest was now nestled neatly in the back, near the barrel that always rubbed his arm. "Da, where am I going to sit?"

"Be quiet," his father hissed. Neither moved. One of the horses began to get uneasy and hoofed at the mud. Roldin wondered what they were waiting for. "There will be only one, for now," the guard had said. It still didn't make any sense to him.

Lost in thought, Roldin almost missed the movement down the road. The moonlight was mostly obscured by thick clouds and the trees that stretched out above him, but he could still just make out something...else... coming their way. Roldin instinctively backed up toward the cart. He tried to climb on but couldn't find a place to squeeze in.

"Da, we should move, something's coming." Roldin said.

"Da? Da!"

His father said nothing. With a morbid fascination, and frozen with fear, the boy watched the something come down the road. It looked like an animal, then the moon vanished behind some clouds and it vanished as well. When the moonlight returned, it looked like a man, but...not. Then it disappeared again.

It seemed to Roldin that the forest was suddenly very, very still. What insect noises he had heard from the trees had gone completely quiet. With bile rising in his throat, the boy was afraid to breathe.

It rose up before him, obscuring every inch of his vision, barreling into him, knocking him to the ground. A hand that was somehow also a claw gripped him by the shoulder tightly and held him motionless deep in the mud. He screamed and struggled, and another hand appeared, covering his mouth, stifling his shrieks. Roldin waited for his father to come to him, to fight this thing off, but his wordless pleas went unanswered.

He was distracted from his panic by attempts to focus on what was on top of him. It seemed to... shift. Sometimes he could see the pre-dawn sky through its skin; other times it was as opaque as rock. It was breathing heavily into his face. Its breath smelled like the inside of a barn in the summer — and felt just as sickly warm — but the hands that gripped him were unbelievably cold. The creature's breathing was ragged and halting, as if it was injured and in pain. Roldin noticed something dark, like ash, falling from its skin and onto his cloak. His eyes widened in shock as a third hand came out of nowhere, tracing a single claw down between his eyes, over his chin, and down his neck. It stopped over his heart.

Roldin could feel his heart...pulled. Despite his manic and muffled screams he was hyperaware of everything happening in slow motion. It felt like something was trying to pull at him from the inside. He could feel the thing's third clawed hand still cold upon his chest, and clearly not inside of him, but the pull was very real. There was pain — sudden and strong— and he cried out in the night despite the second hand that still covered his mouth.

The boy shuddered and found that he could not move. His arms, which had been flailing against his attacker, and his feet, which had been kicking futilely, were still. Neither could he make any further noise. All he could do was watch the creature that crouched over him. As it coalesced into a form that was solid enough he could make out a face. It seemed to have its eyes closed. Its once-labored breathing was now strong as a bellows.

It opened its eyes, red and cold, and regarded him. Then, just as suddenly, it was gone. Vanished. Roldin saw nothing but the cloudy sky above him turning pink and purple through the tree branches as the sun rose somewhere off to his left.

It was beautiful, he couldn't help but think. All he could do was think.

His father was there, finally, standing over him. The bottle was still in his hand. He finished it and tossed it aside. The look on the peddler's face was unreadable. Roldin tried to talk, but he lacked even the strength to move his lips. His feet and hands began to tingle, and he hoped the sharp pins and needles in his toes and fingers meant that he would be able to move them again soon.

"There will be more," his father said. "Six more." Six more what? What was that thing? What happened? Roldin wanted to ask. "You should run, that way," and his father pointed down the road, away from town and into the forest. Why didn't you help me? "I don't know when they will come for you, but they will" What have you done to me? "They won't stop until they get what they want." Why? "You can try to fight them off. Here." His father dropped the prized dagger near Roldin's hand. It fell in the mud next to the boy's useless fingers.

"I'm...sorry?" his father said, as if he was unsure what the phrase meant. "Was just too much coin..." he said with a shrug. With that, the peddler turned to go.

Roldin had feeling in his neck again, and he was able to turn his head as he watched his father climb back on his cart. The man didn't spare a glance toward his son.

"...Da!" he managed to mutter. "Da, come back!" he said hoarsely, with barely enough energy to whisper the plea.

If the peddler had heard, he gave no indication. There wasn't the faintest hint of hesitation in the movement of the cart as it rode passed him, down the road, deeper into the forest.

As the sun climbed in the eastern sky, bathing the world with muted golden hues that peeked through the canopy of the forest, Roldin was alone.

Ransom Prestridge

THE SEVEN SOULS OF
ROLDIN BENIRUS

BOOK ONE
LEGEND OF THE MARKED MAN

THIRTY TWO YEARS LATER

Chapter 1
SOMETIMES, IT'S JUST GAS

The rains fell hard and constant on Mount Everdare. The downpour disturbed the ice-filled crags and snowcaps that had formed after a harsh winter, causing a torrent of mud and rocks and water to flood the small town that lay nestled in the mountain's grey embrace. The residents of Road's End were used to the annual springtime event, and they had long since elevated their houses on stilts, developed a crude plankway system linking houses and other buildings, built up extra-large stores of supplies during the winter, and otherwise learned to live with the yearly inconvenience. Even so, they knew that the spring thaw meant the already quiet town would be even quieter, as the roads connecting them with the rest of the county were cut off and all but impassable to traders, merchants, or anyone who wished to come work the mines until summer's inevitable influx of desperate workers. The thaw, the slides, the sheer quantity of water meant that folks wouldn't find their way to Road's End unless they were hell-bent.

This made it all the more surprising to the townspeople who lounged lazily on covered porches, children who stared forlornly out their windows at the rain, or anyone who happened to be looking down the flooded road to see a figure slogging his way toward the town.

By the time the stranger was staggering his way through the knee-deep mud, approaching the only passage to the main thoroughfare, a half dozen townspeople leaned against the porch railing outside the Goldenpick tavern watching him with fascination.

One of the older gentlemen, a miner in his younger days but now wrinkled with age and regret, spat into the rain and announced, "Those damned mining cart salesmen get bolder every year."

The old woman next to him scoffed. "He wouldn't be selling no mine carts, Silas," she chided. "He's a preacher, no doubt. Come to save our souls and drain our coin for the Sacreds. Just you wait."

"Nah, they know we're all hopeless heathens," a younger, pretty but steely-eyed blonde woman said, wiping flour off of her hands onto her apron. She somehow managed to dust some on the long braid that hung over her shoulder as she flipped it behind herself absently. "He's a tax collector."

"King Twill's tax men came through here last month when the snows were still on the ground, remember, Penny?" Silas nodded to the younger lady. "But I bet he's from the castle. Maybe they want to build a proper road and he's come to survey. That would be a sight, wouldn't it? Would make our tax money finally come to some good use around here, instead of wasting it on whatever in the hells they spend it on. I sure know it doesn't serve me none."

Another man, middle-aged, with an impressive ever-growing belly — and nursing a tall bottle of wine — exited the tavern and cleared his throat. "I heard that, Silas."

The old man had the dignity to only blush slightly. "You know it's true, Mayor Kinnley. If it weren't for the mine, Adren would burn us out like they did Iverdin and

Bear's Crossing last summer."

The mayor took a long swig of his wine and shook his head. "They wouldn't have to, they'd just let us wash away one spring and forget we were ever here." He gestured to the approaching stranger with his chin. "But I do wonder what this one is up to."

The small gathering of men and women resumed watching the solitary man trudge through the rain and mud. He made impressive time, doing a skillful job finding secure footholds and avoiding sinkholes on the flooded road that was covered with a good foot of water and deepening quickly. As he came nearer they could make out a cloak, dark and long, with a hood to keep the rain from his face, and a large pack strapped to his back which seemed well-stocked and bursting at the seams.

"Merchant of some sort, I bet," old man Silas said knowingly. "Bag's probably full of trinkets and, ooh, maybe silks. Bet Penny here could make a pretty dress or two out of it. Something nice and low-cut to wear while she's bending over serving me drinks, right, love?" he said with a lewd chuckle.

Penny lazily tossed a glob of wet flour from her fingers at Silas' face. "I could make you a dress, but I bet you'd look better in suede. Maybe your merchant has that in his packs." The onlookers all gave hearty guffaws to the barmaid — except for Silas, who simply glared at her.

"Is that an...axe?" Mayor Kinnley asked. The townsfolk all squinted at the slowly approaching stranger, and they could indeed make out the weapon, the shaft about two feet long and the large, bearded axe head as black as midnight, hanging from the side of the man's belt.

"Get Jodas, would you?" the mayor prompted one of the younger men who immediately took off, running onto the elevated wooden plank sidewalks that stood precariously above the rushing waters.

As the outsider finished trudging through the muck and finally found his footing on the porch of the tavern, the mayor stood protectively in front of his citizens, his wine bottle abandoned and an impassive look on his face. "You've come a long way, stranger."

The man looked up, his hood still concealing most of his face, and nodded. Rain droplets fell from his cloak in sheets. "That I have," he said with a deep voice. He lifted his hood off his head and wiped rain out of his eyes. He had long brown hair that was sopping wet despite his hood. It was hard to determine his age—somewhere between forty and fifty, maybe. He had dark circles under his eyes and deep creases in his forehead. They could see at least two scars, one across his left cheek leading from the back of his jaw up to his eye, and another claw-like rake of scars on the right side of his neck, barely visible under his hair. His skin was oddly pale for someone who, judging by the pair of well-worn boots on his feet, spent a lot of time on the road. Even so, he was a handsome man, with a strong jaw-line covered in a week's worth of stubble and piercing blue eyes that had the slightest spark of mischief in them. His smile was slight and cocky.

"Sure you're not lost?" the mayor asked.

"Well, I don't usually have a destination," he said with a shrug, and with a well-practiced flair he flicked his cloak behind his right shoulder. The mayor noticed with discomfort that this completely freed the stranger's axe and the arm that could wield it. "So, I suppose me being lost is impossible," he answered with a grin. The mayor and townspeople looked on, not impressed.

The stranger cleared his throat, which gave way to a sudden wracking cough that shook him for a moment. "But, I have come here for a reason, and it is of most dire importance." The man looked up at the sky to spot the setting sun, which was a bare glint against the dark grey clouds above. "Almost dinnertime, if I'm guessing. I wish to address your townspeople in the tavern, if I may. It will only take a moment, but I promise you it is imperative for all to hear."

Loud footsteps bounded down the plankways as the younger man returned with an older one in tow. "There a problem here, mayor?" Jodas asked in a voice that squeaked a little more than he intended. The constable was large in several different ways, wearing a mail vest that didn't quite cover his gut anymore, and a glob of egg on his face that was clearly visible on his ebony skin. The rain made his close-cropped hair sparkle in quite an unintimidating fashion. Jodas gave the stranger an appraising scowl and hefted a long-shanked spear in his hands.

"That's yet to be determined," Kinnley said. He turned back to the outsider. "What do you want to talk to my people about, stranger?"

"Ah, so you're the mayor? Good, good," the man said. "If I may speak to you alone, for one moment?" He gestured to the end of the porch and flashed a disarming smile.

Jodas took a step forward, but the mayor gave a quick shake of his head and joined the stranger. The two men spoke in hushed tones away from the others.

"What do you think he wants?" Silas leaned over and whispered to Penny.

The barmaid shook her head, but there was a queer look on her face as she stared transfixed at the unusual man. "I don't know. I have the oddest feeling that I've seen him somewhere before, but—I don't know." She shrugged and popped a few of her knuckles in frustration. "You can stay here and watch this farce. I'm going to go check on Linder." Penny took off her apron to hold over her head as she bounded away through the rain.

Silas nodded and continued to watch the pair of men converse. He noticed the mayor frown deeply, make a disbelieving hand motion, and shake his head emphatically. The stranger then reached slowly into his pack and brought something out of it that was small and wrapped in cloth. He was speaking while he did so, and as he unveiled the contents the mayor stiffened and took a step back. Then he nodded.

Kinnley walked over to Jodas. The mayor's face was pale. "Wait until sundown and ring the town bell, call out for everyone to gather at the tavern immediately," he said quietly.

Silas frowned, edging closer to the two officials. "What is it?"

"You'll find out soon enough," Kinnley said. He turned to the constable, who was about to voice his own reservations. "Just do it, old friend," he said with a quick shake of his head, then strode purposefully through the rain towards his house.

The stranger was suddenly behind Silas, who jumped in surprise despite himself. The mysterious man begged his pardon and edged his way around Silas and into the tavern. Wull, the barkeep, had been watching the exchange through the window and wrung his hands together as the stranger entered. Silas heard the outsider order a whiskey then saw him hang his cloak on the back of a chair and remove his pack, which hit the boarded floor of the tavern with a heavy thud. With that removed, the old man could see a heavy jacket of mail and scale armor around the stranger's torso. There was a dagger strapped to his belt in addition to the axe, and another smaller dagger on the small of his back.

"By the Sacreds," the old man mumbled. "What kind of battles does this one fight?"

\#

Road's End was a small town, and word traveled fast on gossiping lips when there was nothing else better to talk about. The entire village had gathered in the tavern long before sundown, each pretending to mind their own business, but all eyes and ears were discreetly on the stranger who sat alone at his own table, sipping his second dram of whiskey and wearing an expression that no one could decipher. Wull and Penny worked double time passing out drinks, meat, and bread, and anything else the people asked for as they waited impatiently for whatever the unusual man had to say.

The man himself was saying nothing. He scanned the room slowly, as if looking for something. The candlelight from the table in front of him played off of his blue eyes, making them dance like a couple of silken-clad maidens. His axe had been removed from his belt and was sitting naked on the table in front of him. Its dark blade seemed to suck in the light around it, making it look like there was an axe-shaped hole carved into the tabletop. The mere presence of it seemed to create a whole other level of tension in the tavern.

Most of the citizens were miners — though the mines were still closed due to the spring flooding — and they spent most of their days fishing or swapping stories. The boredom and cabin fever of a long winter stirred the little town into an absolute fervor now that there was actually something happening in Road's End.

The gathered citizens were an odd mix of races from all corners of the lands and everything in between. The outsider noted dark-skinned west islanders, olive-skinned wanderers from the northern wastes, and pale-skinned and blond-haired people from the central nations. Miners of all nationalities went where there was coin to be made, and despite the mix of cultures present, it seemed to the stranger that a kinship had formed in the small town.

Men who were both young enough to still favor flights of fancy and old enough to know better swapped whispered theories with abandon, but old Silas was the biggest stirrer of that pot by far. The tale of the stranger's arrival — which ranged from suddenly appearing on the porch out of thin air to walking on water — was passed around the tavern along with shots of whiskey. The women of the town oscillated between watching him with shy suspicion to batting their eyelashes at him. A couple of the younger girls prodded Penny for any details she knew, but she ignored them. All the while she continued studying the stranger whenever she could spare a moment. Her frown deepened by the minute.

Mayor Kinnley finally strode into the Goldenpick tavern, and, as if on cue, the townsfolk hushed and straightened slightly. Aside a few whispered echoes of lingering conversation, the only sound was the patter of the rain outside.

The mayor nodded to the newcomer a little nervously. "Well, we're all here. Say your piece."

The stranger nodded solemnly and set down his drink. Everyone had tried their best to keep their distance from him — better to spread their gossip without being overheard —so, while the tavern was packed, there was a ring of space radiating from his table very much like a theater stage. The armored man stood and put his hand down on the table next to him, a hands-width away from his axe. No eye in the room could help but glance at it nervously.

"My name," the man said, just loud enough to be heard but also quietly enough that everyone leaned in just a little closer, "is Gaeryn Blackthorn. I've come to you all today with a warning, but also with a promise of hope."

Waves of murmurs spread around the tavern and crashed against each other as each person whispered to their neighbor. Blackthorn waited patiently for the hum to subside before continuing. "I've been tracking something for several days now. It's been out there, hiding in the woods amongst the flooded groves, but I fear it has found what it is looking for and will soon descend upon this peaceful town."

The townspeople's voices grew more worried. The stranger allowed each person time to share theories and I-told-you-this-last-year boasts to the person next to them. Finally they all hushed and looked to Blackthorn expectantly.

"This creature will not be something that is easy to kill. It will be beyond the skill of many of you. If left unchecked to rampage the village, it will surely claim the lives of everyone here."

"A single creature?" someone called out. A chorus of "What could do that?" and "This is nonsense!" spread amongst the gathered throngs. It got loud enough that mayor Kinnley was forced to pat the air in front of him to silence the din.

"The creature that is capable of doing this, the creature that stalks the outskirts of this very town," Blackthorn said, holding the room at his whim for a little longer than he should have, "is a demon."

The whole of the town of Road's End was deathly silent for several heart-stopping moments. Even the constant rain seemed to cease pelting the windows at the dire news from the lips of this mysterious stranger. Then there was a single, loud, inappropriate, brief guffaw that came from Penny, behind the bar. Three dozen sets of eyes turned to her at once to find both hands over her mouth in an attempt to suppress her wide-eyed grin. Then the atmosphere in the tavern exploded in panic.

"Silence, please," Blackthorn said, holding both hands up. Slowly the people regained their composure and stared at him with wide, shining eyes. A hush came over the tavern as every person mulled possibilities in their own heads. "It is frightening, but it is true. Demons," he intoned. The word hovered around him like a threat as he walked slowly around the table. "They can take any shape or form they wish, though they tend to aim for the most vicious-looking—whatever their beastly minds can conjure. They are the fiercest killers known to us. Summoned here by the most foul of your brothers and sisters from a mysterious place no Sacreds can shine, they come to our world to do unspeakable evil."

The entire tavern—save the frowning barmaid—was held captivated. "A single demon, if not slain quickly, has the potential to murder everyone in a whole city, each kill giving it renewed life, vigor, and power, allowing it to stay in our world a little longer... so it can kill again." His low voice echoed off the hearts of those in the room; a dozen legends and folktales they were told as children bounced around inside their heads. "The longest murder spree ever recorded by a demon lasted fifty-two days. A whole nation in the east was annihilated, its name long lost to time. Only ruins remain." The room seemed to grow colder by the moment.

"I promise you, citizens of...of..." he seemed to flounder for a moment until someone in the front row prompted him, "Road's End. I promise you, citizens of Road's End, that I will let no harm come to you. I am more than just a traveler. I am a demon slayer of famed repute. Some of you probably have heard my name," he said, and a few heads nodded in sudden realization. "I know what is hunting you, and with this knowledge I will protect this village, or give my life trying."

"What does it want?" someone called out. "Why is it here?" another chimed in.

"It has come," he said, and scanned the room one more quick time, his eyes again finding what he was looking for, "for her." His finger pointed to the end of the bar, where a trio of young ladies stood huddled together in terror. All three jumped in unison.

"For...for me?" asked one, a skinny girl wearing a tight-fitting bonnet over her thin hair and revealing a mouth full of crooked teeth behind her horrified gape.

"No, no," Blackthorn said quickly, "the one in the green dress next to you." A buxom girl of about seventeen, her raven hair flowing down her shoulders like an ebon waterfall hugging a face delicately made up with rosy cheeks and red lips, put her hand to her ample chest and swooned slightly. Her two friends to either side caught her and began fanning her vigorously. There was an ocean of gasps in the room.

"I promise no harm will come to this girl," Blackthorn declared, his hand raised in a determined fist.

"What can you do?" someone wailed. "What hope do we have?"

"I will let this demon come, root it out of its hiding place," he said in a strong baritone. "I have killed countless demons in my years walking this world. None have defeated me, and all have fallen before me like wheat for the harvest. When the demon comes for the girl I will tear its black heartstone from its chest and rend it asunder with my axe, this I swear to you!" He reached back and picked up his weapon, holding it aloft. As one, the room cheered in sudden, exasperated relief at the display of bravado in front of them. One woman fainted and had to be supported by her husband, who still cheered with his free fist.

"All I ask," he said as the room regained its composure, "is enough coin to cover my travels, a roof over my head while I wait for the beast to strike — and for whatever time I need to recover afterwards— and your unwavering trust. This last is most important," Blackthorn said gravely, bowing his head in deference to his audience. They all mumbled their agreements as one, Mayor Kinnley loudest amongst them. "This tavern, I believe, is as good a place as any. I will stay here and wait for the beast."

The townsfolk began tittering nervously, looking at windows and out of the open door of the tavern, though they could see nothing beyond the curtains of rain. Blackthorn replaced the axe on the tabletop and raised his head to take in the room around him, his deep voice wafting over the frightened crowd like a reassuring blanket. "I will begin my vigil of protection. It is best, now, that you all retreat to your homes. Lock your doors. It shall be a long night."

The village began to leave, slowly, none eager to go out into the rain. Blackthorn raised his hand to the girl in green, who was being hugged fiercely by her parents. "My lady," he said with a bow, "I meant every word I said. I hate to endanger you like this, but it would be safest if you would stay with me. The closer you are to me, the safer you will be when the time comes."

Her parents' faces fell, but the brave girl stood up straight, her chest heaving in slightly-panicked breaths, and nodded. She turned to her parents, "I probably will be safer here," she said with a smile, though her voice trembled. "I don't want to put you two in danger…"

They hugged their daughter again, and her father approached Blackthorn and clasped his arm tightly.

"Protect my little girl," he said. "She's the best of us."

"I give you my word as a man of honor," the stranger said and returned the clasp with a nod.

One by one the tavern emptied, and the sounds of dozens of feet running a little faster than usual through the rain echoed on the wooden plank walkways of Road's End. Soon it was just Blackthorn, the frightened girl, and Penny, the barmaid.

The warrior sauntered up to the bar and gave Penny a solemn bow of greeting. "It's best if you head home, too, my lady barkeep. It won't be safe for much longer." He then motioned to the girl, who sat at his table huddled in his cloak. "But, before you go, a bottle of whiskey, if you please," he said quietly. "I'm sure mayor Kinnley would approve if it went on a tab?" He looked back at the girl, whose tears ran in dark rivets through her makeup, and then turned back to Penny. "Can you make it two?"

Penny said nothing, instead just staring at him, her head tilted to one side. Without taking her eyes off of him she reached down and picked up a bottle of the house's finest and uncorked it, then a second, placing both between them. Blackthorn's hand reached out to grasp one, but the barmaid held fast onto it.

"You," she said, with a growing smile on her lips, "are so unbelievably full of shit."

"Pardon?" Blackthorn asked, unable to hide the surprise on his face.

"You are, you're full of it and you know it!" she exclaimed. The stranger put his finger to his lips to quiet her. The girl behind them, encompassed by the man's cloak and shivering slightly, seemed not to be paying attention.

"You're trying to scare that poor girl and everyone

else here. You should be ashamed of yourself!" she chided in a piercing whisper.

"I assure you, lady barmaid, what I say is true." He pointed outside the door of the tavern. "Any minute now a demon is going to come through that door and try to feast on that girl's blood, and I will kill it like I have countless others. I do what I do to protect this town, and this girl!"

Penny was shaking her head. "You do what you do to scam this town, and this girl. And I know it!"

Blackthorn put his hands on the bar and took a steadying breath. "My lady, how many demons have you met in your life, hmm?" he asked quietly. "How many have you slain? I could tell you my story but we don't have that kind of time. I could show you horrors in my pack over there that would turn—your—hair—white." He sighed. "Besides, what would I be getting out of lying to the noble town of Stone's End?"

"Road's End," Penny corrected.

"Of course."

The barmaid nodded her head, her smirk getting wider. "Oh I know exactly what you'll be getting out of it. You get to play the hero and stay close to the pretty young girl over there. You're going to offer to hold her," she hugged her arms around herself and feigned a relieved smile, "to comfort her, while the minutes tick by and the night grows colder as she waits for fate to catch up to her. You'll get her fawning over your words, get her to feel safe and protected by this hero out of a maiden's fantasy, and oops!" She held her hands up in the air in a shrug, "you've suddenly tripped and fallen into her nethers! What a shame. Oh, looks like the demon's late! You'll get paid for your vigil tomorrow, say you must have scared it off, and you'll go. Simple as that. So..." she said, her grin growing wicked and her eyes hard, "tell me I'm wrong."

Blackthorn took a deep breath and shook his head. "If you want to stay here and watch me all night, you can. I won't touch the girl. But there will be a demon coming through that door —"

"Nope, no there won't," Penny said, shaking her head, her arms crossed.

The demon slayer blinked at her. "Yes, there will."

"No, there won't."

"Yes, there will!"

"Nope. Ask me," she said, leaning in close, a gleeful chuckle growing in the back of her throat. "Ask me how I know. Come on…ask me…"

"This is absurd."

"Not even a little bit. Come on," she repeated, squinting at the warrior across the bar from her. "Ask me how I know about your little game, you rogue."

Blackthorn paused. "How do you —"

"Because you did it to *me* eight years ago!" she growled and poked him in his chest.

"I — what?"

"You did! I thought I recognized you when you waltzed into town. You have a new name, though, and a slightly different story. You're a lot older-looking than you used to be. But I remember your face. I remember that swagger, that greasy charm." Her grin turned into a sneer. "You don't even remember me, do you?"

"Listen, there must be some mistake."

She gasped. "You don't! You honestly don't. Let me paint you a picture, then." She leaned further across the bar and Blackthorn took a sudden step back from her glare. "Town of Levin's Ferry. Fall. Eight years ago. You came into town, started asking questions to the guards, asked if anything's been spotted in the wilderness nearby. The mayor gets wind of it, seeks you out, you tell him you think a demon's on the loose and is coming for — hold-on-let-me-find-the-prettiest-girl-in-town — this little blonde one right here." Penny pointed at herself with her thumbs. "I was only eighteen, you monster. I was young and pretty and naïve...I spent the night with you in the tavern, sure my doom would come, sure my life was over and I wouldn't get to do all the things I wanted to do. And you had your strong hands, and your pretty eyes, and told me life is too short for everyone and blah, blah, blah —" a fierceness choked her voice. "Don't you make me *remember* the choices I made that night!"

Penny took one of the bottles of whiskey on the bar and drank deep from it. "But guess what? It never came. You stayed for three damned days, getting drunk every night, keeping me scared out of my mind, then you left the fourth morning claiming the danger was over. No one knew what had happened and they all thought I had something to do with it!"

Blackthorn shook his head in disbelief, as, quite suddenly, realization dawned. "Levin's Ferry?" Penny nodded. "Is that...is that the town with the giant mill and that pretty stone bridge in the middle?" She nodded again. "Oh — ohhhhh — right. You know, there was a demon out there, but there was another demon slayer lurking around that part of the woods, too. She ended up killing it first, and —"

He was interrupted by a mighty slap from the barmaid.

"Don't even start," she sneered. "I could tell you about what happened to me and my reputation after that, but it would turn—your—face—red. *If* you had any shame left in your soul, which I doubt." The barmaid crossed her arms and stood tall. "So, I'm going to be staying with you tonight to make sure what happened to me doesn't happen to that girl over there. And, anyway, this tavern is mine," she said with a glare in her eyes, and then shrugged. "Well, half mine, but I'll be damned if that half gets trashed by a charlatan."

"Which half is yours?"

"The pretty half," she deadpanned through dangerously narrowing eyes. Penny gestured to the girl in the back. "Do you even know how young she is?"

Blackthorn began to shrug and voice an argument, but swallowed it, suddenly distracted. His head whipped around to the door, then up to the ceiling, then back to a window.

"What are you playing at?" Penny asked with a shake of her head.

The slayer held a hand up to quiet her and slowly backed away to his table, where he grabbed his axe. The buxom young girl, still lost in her reverie, jumped when he got near, and her eyes went wide when she saw the weapon in his hand.

"Stop it," the barmaid chided.

Blackthorn quietly stepped into the center of the tavern and put a hand over his stomach. "Something's...I think," he said softly, mostly to himself, shaking his head. "Hard to tell anymore. Takes a lot to terrify me these days. Sometimes, it's just gas, but..."

"I dare you to be sick on my floor."

He faced the door again. Penny peered out, and saw nothing but rain in the blackness.

All the candles in the tavern, even the fireplace on its side wall, flickered as a gust of wind barreled through the open door. All the windows were forced open from the outside. A few of them shattered. The girl in green screamed, stood up from her chair, then fainted and slumped back down to the ground.

The demon slayer laughed abruptly, looking very relieved, and pointed a gauntleted finger at the barmaid. "Hah! I told you!"

A figure from a nightmare completely blocked the doorway. It was covered in cobalt blue scales from head to toe, with tall horns jutting from its head, and spikes of razor points poking out randomly throughout its body. Two giant, bat-like wings trailed behind the creature. As it hulked in the doorway, they seemed to fold up and in on themselves, vanishing as quickly as thought, leaving rain drops falling from the space that they had just inhabited.

It entered the tavern deliberately, a claw-tipped talon bracing the doorway as it did so, leaving deep gouges in the wood. Small red eyes scanned the room and came to rest on the demon slayer standing in the center. A maw full of fangs seemed to curve into a smile. "Roldiiiiiiiin…" it growled, like distant thunder.

"Zhannavirik, I thought I smelled you," the demon slayer sneered. Without another word the two figures rushed each other. Penny backed away and crouched down behind the bar; only her eyes and hair remained visible as she watched the clash begin.

There was a crashing sound as flesh and scales met. The slayer's axe swung at one of the horns, but the demon was too quick and ducked underneath. It lashed out with a claw but Roldin backed away once, twice, three times as the creature swung wildly, barely missing his foe. A fourth time it reached out and grabbed the slayer's axe. As swift as a fox, Roldin brought out a dagger with his left hand and impaled the scaled arm that held his axe fast. It twitched but kept its grip. The slayer twisted the dagger and kicked at one of the thing's scaled legs. Its knee buckled, and Roldin released his first dagger and unsheathed a second from his back, slashing the demon twice on the chest. The strikes bounced off of its scales. The slayer kicked again, this time directly in the hulking center of mass, and the demon fell back, releasing its grip.

It recovered quickly, rolling up into a crouch. It removed the dagger from its arm and threw the blade on the floor with a clang. Penny thought she could see the thing's legs morph from those of a man's to those of a cat's, and with a growl the demon leapt an impossible distance through the air and barreled into its opponent. Roldin crouched and, using the demon's momentum, allowed himself to fall on his back, launching the beast into the air with his legs.

The demon's claws seemed to extend and it latched itself onto the ceiling rafters with all four appendages. Its head swiveled at an angle that heads aren't supposed to turn and it looked at Roldin with venom in its red eyes. With amazing speed it crawled, upside down, from rafter to rafter, avoiding Roldin's axe and snapping its teeth as it went.

Its wings returned and flapped once, sending the slayer flying backward into the wall with a grunt. The demon released its grip on the ceiling and twisted, falling, catlike, into a crouch. The wings once again vanished suddenly. It leapt again at Roldin. This time, the demon slayer ducked, rolling out of the way, and the creature slammed into the wall, dazing itself.

Roldin backed away, switching his axe to his left hand, and with his right he reached out to grab one of the bottles of whiskey off the bar. As the demon turned to face him, shaking its head, Roldin took one quick swig, and...waited. The thing growled — a sound that shook the cups and glass bottles around the tavern — and lunged forward.

The demon slayer threw the bottle. The creature lifted its arm, easily blocking the toss successfully, but the alcohol and glass shards covered its scales. Roldin gripped his axe in both hands and anticipating the demon's next move. As it lashed out, the slayer turned and caught its outstretched arm under the hook of his bearded axe in one fluid motion. With the demon's arm trapped, Roldin stooped down on one knee, twisting in a direction that the creature's arm was not meant to go, and forced the demon to twirl around. He spun the creature once then twisted the axe to free the demon's arm. Finally, the warrior kicked it squarely in the chest, sending it falling back into the fireplace.

The whiskey immediately went up in flames. The demon shrieked, initially patting itself with its claws, trying to combat the hungry flames. Then Penny thought she saw its skin change. The scales disappeared, and, with them, the burning whiskey-soaked fire. The demon laughed, even as its soft cobalt flesh was exposed.

The demon slayer took every advantage.

He lashed out with his axe, biting into the demon's shoulder, then the skin of its belly, then slashing across its back as it turned to flee. With every strike, more dark blue smoke rushed out from its body, only for scales to appear, covering the wounds, as if the demon was reacting defensively — but always just a second too late.

The creature was weakening.

Roldin gripped the axe at either end, wrapping it around the demon's throat from behind, choking it with the two-foot wooden haft. The creature's arms grabbed at the axe but both combatants were capable of remarkable strength. Abruptly, the demon grew a tail barbed with a foot-long spike and impaled Roldin in his upper left thigh.

The slayer's leg buckled, but he didn't release his grip. The demon struggled, gasping for air. Penny wasn't quite sure what she saw next: one moment the demon's head was in a vise, and the next it was re-appearing out of the middle of its back and biting out at Roldin's chest. The demon slayer smiled wanly. Dropping his left hand from his axe, he punched the misplaced head. He then aimed a swing of his axe where the demon's head used to be. Penny squinted as the demon regrew its head, snapping forward to bite Roldin's neck with its fangs, instead, connecting with Roldin's well-place axe swing. It exploded in a dark mess of smoke and ash.

The demon fell to the floor. Its body seemed to shimmer in spasms, with scales growing randomly in some places, spikes in others, and even small wings sprouting here and there — as if it were in a panic. Roldin lifted his axe high above his head and brought it down on the partially scaled chest, meeting the dark blue scales with a dull thud. He brought the axe up again, chipping off more scales on his second hack. A third would most surely cut the thing in half.

The demon's clawed hand raised to catch the axe in its grip. Yet another head seemed to re-form from the ruins of the old one, and it snarled as its other hand reached up, grabbed Roldin's mail armor at the neck, and pulled. It forced the demon slayer on the ground, and the creature rolled to pin him to the floor by his shoulders. Its maw was inches away from the man's face. Its long, spiked tail curled around and hovered menacingly, inches from his eyes, dancing around his face and managing to cut a small gash across his forehead.

"Is this any way to treat an old friend, Zhanny?" Roldin struggled to say.

The demon brought one hand down over Roldin's chest and made a pulling motion with its claws. "You are mine now, Rolidiiin," it sneered, drawing out the man's name with a guttural growl.

Roldin's eyes went wide. He thrashed under the pain and the weight of the demon on top of him. "None. Of. That!" the slayer cried, and wriggled a glass vial of something off of his belt with the part of his arm that wasn't pinned. It seemed to Penny it was full of water, but when he crushed the glass against the demon's torso, breaking the vial, the creature screamed in agony and sat up. Roldin maneuvered both legs to kick it away, sending the demon sprawling.

Penny could see the demon slayer crawl across the floor of the bar until he retrieved his axe. He regained his feet, limping where the tail barb had pierced his thigh. With an almost primal yell, Roldin rushed forward — as much as he could with his injured leg — and brought the axe around with both hands, cleaving the same spot on the demon's chest where he had broken the vial. Its scales seemed to be weakened by the water and they cracked easily at the blow. The demon slayer left his axe buried in the demon's chest, freeing both hands to grip the creature by its neck in a stranglehold.

It then seemed to find its strength. The tail whipped around again, tripping the demon slayer. Roldin lurched but caught himself with one hand on the bar. With his other hand, he grabbed the protruding axe. With a mighty yell, he and the demon spun around in a morbid dance, the slayer gripping the axe and the demon gripping the man. The creature gained the advantage and lifted Roldin, slamming the man down on the bar. He hit the wood with an agonizing crash, knocking bottles and glasses all around. Penny yelped and backed away. She turned and took the golden-plated mining pick —the relic that gave the tavern its name — off of the wall. Clasping it tightly with both hands, she slammed it down onto the demon's back.

The pick managed to lodge itself into its scales and the demon let out a shriek. As it turned to reach out for Penny, Roldin kicked up with his good leg and caught the demon on the back of its head, surprising it and sending it reeling back. Roldin reached out to grab again at the axe that was still lodged inside the demon. He pulled, freeing it. Thick, dark smoke billowed in small waves. The slayer found his feet and leapt off the bar, chopping downward. He took off a leg at a joint, then hewed again at an outstretched arm. Finally, he swung again at its smoking chest, rending scales and flesh alike and leaving a gaping wound. The demon staggered and fell to the ground. It tore the axe away from Roldin as it fell and threw the weapon across the tavern.

Roldin stepped too hard on his injured leg without meaning to and fell. As he hit the floor, he could see the creature twisting in agony, but also saw it slowly recovering its wits. He did not have much time. The slayer cast about and discovered the dagger on the floor where the demon had hurled it. He hurried to grab the blade then hobbled over to the fallen demon.

Bracing his left hand against the gaping wound in its chest, he found his target and brought his dagger down. Penny heard a clinking sound, like metal hitting stone. Still the demon writhed. Roldin lifted the dagger again and brought it down with a grunt. She could hear the sound of metal breaking.

The beast reached up then, clawing its way up Roldin's arm bringing its menacing jaws to his throat. The demon slayer saw the glint of the golden pick sticking out from its back. He reached over the snarling face for the handle and wrenched the pick painfully free. Leaning in with all his weight, he pushed the demon back down with his left hand, swinging the golden pick with his right, as if mining for the most precious metals found only in the creature's chest. This time, Penny heard the sound of stone shattering.

The demon convulsed in a spasm of dark, blue smoke that wafted from its body in all directions like a sudden strong gust of wind, blowing out the candles — and the fire in the fireplace — completely. The dank, acrid smoke hugged the shadows in the tavern common room until it seemed to simply melt into the dark corners.

Penny's eyes were wide, straining to see anything in the sudden darkness. A hand reached out from the other side of the bar. She jumped with a gasp, but found herself thankful it looked human. Roldin lifted himself up from the floor, blood dripping from a gash on his scalp, and shook his head. He took the last bottle of whiskey that lay on its side — most of its contents spilled across the bar — finished what little remained in it, and wiped his mouth.

"I told you," he repeated, and passed out.

CHAPTER 2

AN OLD COMPLAINT

Roldin was floating.

He looked down and saw a yawning chasm far below him; his feet dangled in empty air. The horizon stretched out before him, thick as soup and red as blood, but no land was in sight.

The demon slayer tried to roll his eyes at the banality of the setting and noticed he seemed to be missing his eyelids. He moved his hands in front of his face to shield his eyes from the scarlet glare around him. The oozing pinprick in his left hand had been turned into a hole so large that he could see straight through it. The sky beyond churned and a freezing breeze began to cut through what remained of his soul

"You should open your eyes, Roldin," a voice said, carried by the wind. The feminine voice was hollow and sultry — and instantly recognizable.

"You have to do better than this, Yunirax," Roldin responded. His own voice sounded muffled. "Your little dreams scared me as a child but I don't respond to your parlor tricks anymore."

The voice attempted to laugh, emitting a strained cackle instead. "Your squeals were so delightful back then, weren't they?" it purred. "You've grown over the years but you don't use your body as you should. Your feet do not walk where they ought to, your ears do not hear…" The red sky around him pulsated with a bright red light that burned his un-closable eyes, "…and your eyes do not see."

Roldin knew none of this was real, knew that the pain in his eyes was imagined, but it was uncomfortable all the same. "Riddles? You bother Ryufalin to torment me with riddles?"

"And why not?" the voice taunted. "You're still a riddle to me. We've been chasing you for a long time and you've slipped through our fingers repeatedly, despite our best efforts. Do not think you can evade us, forever. We will take what is rightfully ours…what is rightfully mine."

"My soul is still my own, Yunirax, while I hold it within me."

"For now." The cold air around him shifted violently, carrying him up in a slipstream. The wind rushed into his lungs and his stomach lurched towards his feet. Just as quickly, the carrying winds vanished, and Roldin began to plummet. The red skies above receded but no ground rose up to meet him—just an inky blackness of nothing.

The voiced returned to him, louder, almost shrieking as he fell. "What I want to know is, has the boy grown up to be his father? Could the boy who became a man through such pain cause another to know the same?"

"NEVER!" Roldin yelled out into the nothing. He had the uneasy feeling that the ground was finally going to sprint toward him at any moment, but, even with un-closable eyes, he could not see it coming.

"We shall see…" the voice whispered menacingly, "Open your eyes, boy…"

Roldin woke up to the sound of his own coughing. It

was a rude awakening, shaking the slayer out of his fitful sleep, but one he was used to. He rolled over to clear his lungs and quickly realized he was in a bed — instead of floating in a sea of red — and he froze to evaluate his surroundings. Roldin blinked, momentarily relieved to notice his eyelids were just where they should be, and surveyed the room. He relaxed a little when he saw his axe, his remaining dagger, his armor, and his bag, neatly piled on the table next to him.

Across the room was an old woman with her back to him, pouring steaming liquid into a cup. She turned, her wrinkled face wearing a patient smile, and walked over to his bed with the hot drink. "Sip this, for your cough," she said sweetly. "You've been coughing and thrashing all night."

Roldin nodded, rubbing his aching eyes and was thankful again for his eyelids. He took the cup, which smelled of mint and darkroot, from the lady with a smile. "Thank you," he said, "but this won't do much. It's an old complaint." He sipped at it anyway.

Scanning the room, he decided that he was in some kind of medicine hut. Jars upon jars of herbs lined the walls, with fresher bunches tied, hanging by strings from the ceiling to dry. The small one-roomed hut smelled like dirt and plants; a smell the wilderness-wandering slayer found familiar. The medicine woman sat down and fussed with the dressing on his leg. "It's still warm, but less swollen. I don't...I don't know what that demon stabbed you with, but it certainly doesn't agree with you. I'd keep an eye on it if I were you." The slayer nodded his thanks as she gestured upward. "I couldn't seem to do much for that wound on your hand, either."

He raised his left hand and saw a bandage around it, too. Roldin carefully pulled it back and saw the familiar pin-prick of sticky dried blood in the middle of his palm, still bleeding stubbornly even after thirty years. "This is an even older complaint," he explained with a sad smile, "and there's definitely not much anyone can do for this."

The old woman stood and adjusted the blanket around Roldin. "Well the whole town is singing your praises — how you saved us last night. It's quite something to have a genuine hero here in Road's End. My name is Nanny, but everyone just calls me 'Old Nanny' — though not to my face. Can't imagine why," she said with a wry grin. "Now, you get as much rest as you need. I'll be back with some lunch, later."

She left him. Roldin finished his cup of tea and lay back on the pillow. He placed his hands contentedly over his chest and breathed deeply; trying to relax, trying to sleep. His slow inward breath ended in another coughing fit and a frustrated sigh.

The demon slayer forced his eyes closed again. At the bitter edge of fatigue, images swam before his closed eyes, unbidden: nights spent hiding in the woods when he was a child…days spent walking down a road, any road, one foot in front of the other, always moving…nights spent running…days spent fighting for his life, for his soul. His clenching hands were callused where they had spent a lifetime around an axe handle, and he could feel his blisters throb in time with his pulse as his heart began to beat faster and faster. Demons formed in front of his closed eyes, horrors of every kind imaginable. He replayed battle after battle in his memories. He lost feeling in his fingers and toes again, as sensation was replaced by a hollow pain that he couldn't shake. He could feel the black ash of thousands of demons cover his hands and his face, choking him. Red, human blood poured from somewhere above and soaked into the demon ash. The mixture swelled into a waterfall that didn't end, that would not end, that could not end. The blood cascaded over his face, covering his mouth and his nose. He was drowning…

He may have slept for an instant, he wasn't sure. Sweat beaded his forehead and his chest felt as if his heart was trying to escape. He knew that the dream had been of his own making— he didn't need demon influence to give himself nightmares. The blanket the old woman had fit snugly around him felt very much like a vise, and he kicked it off quickly with his good leg. Roldin sat up, swinging himself around, putting as little weight on his left thigh as he could. He gripped his hair tightly and wrenched. He squeezed his eyes shut, pulled his head down, and faced the floor. His breaths came in gasps. The feeling of his scalp being torn pulled him —slowly— back to reality. Tears tried to form in his eyes but he wouldn't let them. Not now. Not ever.

He was able to gradually gain control of his breathing. Quickly inhale, slowly exhale. Roldin let go the grip on his hair and combed his fingers through it to straighten it out.

"That's enough sitting still for one day," he muttered to himself when his panic had finally left him.

His eyes were tired, but they always were, and he knew sleep would not comfort him today. He saw a crutch that must have been set aside for him. It was plain but sturdy— which was all he needed. It would serve well enough. He retrieved some plain clothes from his pack and carefully pulled the trousers on over his bandaged leg. His dark, soft cotton tunic was loose-fitting and comfortable. He fished a dry cloak from his pack and shook it out. Lastly, he strapped his axe onto his belt.

Roldin tried limping around the house with the crutch. It helped, but it was slow. Very slow.

Roldin Benirus was never slow.

The rain had abated to a calm drizzle. As he opened the door to the hut, the soft glow of a cloud-covered midmorning sun welcomed him—along with about a dozen villagers who had been milling around outside. They all turned his way and cheered as he emerged. He drank in their praises and their thanks, received handshakes from the men and kisses from the women. A couple of young boys crowded around his legs, trying to get a good look at his axe. One ran off boasting to others that he had touched it and that it froze his hand and that it would never work again, but that was alright because the axe was magic and it was worth it.

One of the older boys mustered up enough nerve to talk to him. "Why do you use an axe?" he asked. "All the heroes in the stories fight with swords!" A small gaggle of children gathered behind the older one, intent on the demon slayer's response.

Roldin felt the eyes of a few adults — likely their parents —and he chose his words carefully. "Axes are more functional than swords. With this axe I can also fell a tree, cut firewood, clear underbrush, and do all kinds of things that I need to do in the forest to survive. It's a tool just as much as it is a weapon." The children deflated a little. Roldin sighed—he couldn't stand the sight of a sad child. "And it really splinters scales or anything else a demon conjures to protect itself which makes it easier to crack its heartstone and banish it to the evil realm from whence it came," he said quickly. The children all jumped up and down and cheered, whooping excitedly.

Mayor Kinnley worked his way through the crowd that was singing his praises. The mayor himself swore platitudes and promises of coin, but Roldin had heard talk like that many times before. Distracted, he kept scanning the crowd for one person in particular, but he didn't see her.

"Ah, I know what you're looking for," the mayor said with a wink, and turned around. The young girl in green, who was wearing white today, stepped forward, shyly kissed Roldin on the cheek, and hugged him tightly as her crying parents looked on, holding each other. She was introduced to him as Clariya, and the demon slayer bowed before her and tried to act graceful. Her father approached Roldin and promised him anything, anything at all. The slayer thought he saw Clariya pale a little at that. He reassured her —and her father —that nothing else was required, he was simply doing his job.

Discreetly, he continued scanning the crowd, as she was not the one he was looking for. The mayor interrupted his search and declared that there would be a large feast in the tavern that night in celebration of the victory. Roldin bowed his head and said he wouldn't miss it, and a cheer went up.

Eventually the novelty wore off and the crowd began to dissipate. When Roldin was finally able to tear himself away from the lingerers, it was almost noon. The rain was falling a little harder. He pulled the hood of his cloak around his head and was careful as he hobbled through the town, trying his best not to let the end of the crutch get stuck in any gaps in the plankways.

The town itself was not large. It consisted of three parallel streets with wooden buildings on either side of each, packed in tightly together. The roads were still flooded, meaning the town was divided by three decently sized rivers, but the high walkways and rope bridges kept it well connected. The tavern was all the way back on the far northwest street from where he was, and it was a slow trip over. Along his walk he could see where the road — now a river—came in from the forest to the West and forked into three at the town, then ended at the far Eastern end of the village where the currently flooded mines dug deep into Mount Everdare.

When he got to the tavern, he saw the other barkeep

still cleaning up the mess from the night before. A couple of men were installing new windows, and a third was repairing a few cracks in the wooden wall and bar. They seemed to bear him no ill will for the damage, though.

"Happy to have you back, Blackthorn, sir," Wull said with a bow and nervously wiped his brow. "I'm afraid that my stock is being replenished out of our stores right now, with the majority of that being saved for the festivities tonight…"

"That's quite all right," Roldin said with a smile. "Actually, I was looking for the barmaid that was with me last night. Is she around?"

"Oh, you mean Penny? I believe she's at home right now. She lives on the far side of the third street over, at the end, a little bit off the street proper, house nearest the tree line."

Of course, on the completely opposite side of town Roldin thought to himself, his leg already throbbing in protest. "Thank you. I just wanted to…thank her for her help last night. She was very brave."

"Ah, well, that's wonderful, wonderful."

Roldin turned to go but Wull touched his shoulder lightly. "Oh, sir, if you could, um…" He backed away and bent down to remove a napkin that had been placed on the floor. Underneath, with a deep gash in the center where the mining pick had pierced it, were the remains of the demon's heartstone. Wull backed away from it quickly and wiped his brow again. "Everyone was afraid to touch it, but we figured you would know the safest way to dispose of it properly?"

"Of course, I'd be happy to," Roldin said. He stepped over to the stone, then paused and looked up at Wull and the other workers who had craned their necks to get a look at the slayer in action. "If you all wouldn't mind looking away? Demon slayer trade secret and all that." Wull jumped and practically spun around. The other men nodded knowingly and turned their heads—that way they couldn't see Roldin scrunch up his face in pain and nearly lose his balance as he bent over quickly, snatched up the pieces, and put it all in the pocket of his trousers. "It is done. The area is now cleansed," he intoned solemnly. One of the workers took off his hat and held it over his heart in reverence.

Roldin's leg felt like it was on fire by the time he made it to Penny's house. It was where Wull described it, a little off to the side of the town proper, down a longer walkway, nestled in a little stand of trees. It wasn't overly large but also not too small. A cozy waft of smoke rose up from the chimney and an inviting light shone from a window, fighting back the rainy-day gloom. The slayer limped up to the doorway, balanced himself, and knocked. After a moment the door opened— but he didn't see anyone. He had to look down and came face to face with a little boy, who regarded him curiously with large, blue eyes.

"Hello," Roldin said after a moment.

"Hello," the boy replied.

"I'm looking for Penny—your mother?" he asked. The boy nodded. "Is she home?"

"No," he said.

Roldin put on his most disarming smile. "My name is Gaeryn. I'm a friend of your mother's. Will she be back soon?" The boy nodded. "Can I come in and wait for her?" The storm was getting stronger by the minute and his cloak was already drenched.

The boy regarded him very suspiciously for a moment, and seemed to deliberate. "All right," he finally said. He backed away and let Roldin inside. The home was indeed small — only about three rooms, from what he could see — but the fireplace was warm and inviting and, with a few fluffy pillows and blankets surrounding it, ready for snuggling. The walls were hung with warm blankets and cheery candles. Here and there, pieces of parchment with drawings decorated the main room. There were two shelves overflowing with books and a kitchen with a large window that let in as much light as would show through the constant clouds. Roldin took a deep breath and grinned as the smell of warm bread filled the air.

"You have to dry off over there," the boy said and pointed to a corner of the house with a carpet laid out. "Ma says so."

The demon slayer obeyed, removing his boots and holding his cloak to let it drip onto the carpet. The boy kept watching him. "What happened to your leg?" he asked.

Roldin opened his mouth to respond, then decided better of it and cleared his throat instead. He continued to wring out his cloak. "I tripped, fell. I'm clumsy like that."

The boy nodded. "I fall sometimes too. Last spring I fell off into the river."

Roldin raised his eyebrows. "That must have been scary."

"It wasn't so bad. It's not so deep, and the other boys play in it sometimes, though the adults say it's dangerous. Ma won't let me — unless I fall in."

"It probably is dangerous," Roldin offered. "So, how often do you fall in on purpose?" The boy didn't answer, but he began to smirk.

The demon slayer grinned back and hung his cloak on a peg on the wall. "What's your name?"

"Linder," the boy replied.

"Nice to meet you."

Linder smiled, then his eyes wandered to the weapon on Roldin's belt. The boy stiffened. "This is nothing for you to worry about," Roldin said. "I just use it for firewood." The man took his belt and axe off and placed both with his cloak.

"Can I sit over here?" he asked, gesturing to a chair nestled near a small kitchen table. The boy nodded and watched as Roldin limped to the chair, pulled it out, and struggled trying to find a comfortable way to sit down. Linder regarded him for a moment, then sat in a chair opposite the demon slayer, picked up a book on the table, and began to read.

Roldin politely sat in silence and was content to explore the house with his eyes. After a while he couldn't help but tilt his head sideways to read the title of the story the boy was reading. "That's a good book," he said. "I read it when I was your age."

Linder stopped reading and looked up at him in surprise. "You've read this book?" Roldin nodded. "How does it end?" he asked quickly.

"I—what? Why don't you just read it?"

"I want to know how it ends."

Roldin hesitated then made a face. "Well, I mean, it'll make more sense if you read the whole thing. If you're so eager to know, why don't you just skip to the ending?"

"Ma tore out the last few pages," Linder said sadly.

"She—why would she do a thing like that?" Roldin asked, confused.

"Because I always skip to the end. Ma wanted me to stop doing it so she makes me read all of this, then she'll give me the last pages." Linder looked down at the book with a frown.

"Would you not read it if you knew the ending?" Roldin asked.

"I would. I would just feel better if I knew it had a happy ending. Can you just tell me?"

"Well..." Roldin studied the boy. Linder stared at him intently with pleading eyes. "Sometimes, books are sad. They can still be good, but, just like life, stories can be sad. But that doesn't mean they're not worth reading."

"How can a good story have a sad ending?"

Roldin paused and exhaled sharply with a shrug. "I suppose it's not all about the ending. A story isn't just made up of an ending—a good book is about walking the road, not just where you end up."

Linder seemed to consider this. "But a happy ending makes me feel happy afterwards. A sad ending makes me feel bad. I don't want to spend all day reading a book if it's just going to make me sad."

Roldin scratched his stubble in thought. "Do you like pie?" he asked. The boy nodded emphatically. "Pie is good, right? And eating it is fun?" Linder nodded again. "But once you eat it, it's gone. Isn't that sad?"

Linder's face scrunched up as he thought about it. "What if I can have another piece?"

"You just ate the last one."

"That is pretty sad."

Roldin nodded. "And even though it's sad that your pie is gone, it was still worth eating it, and it doesn't make eating it less enjoyable, does it? That's why a good book can be sad, but still be good."

Linder thought for a long time. "I don't think reading a book is really like eating pie."

The demon slayer cleared his throat. "Yes, well, you just can't read the end of a book first. You have to earn it by eating—I mean reading— the rest of it. It's what the storyteller intended."

The boy shook his head. "I don't know the writer and they don't know I'm reading it. Why can't I just know the end first?"

Roldin threw up his hands. "Because—we'll, you just can't. You shouldn't, anyway. When you do that you're cheating, you know."

"I'm not a cheater!"

"Of course you're not, because Ma tore out the last few pages, eh?"

Linder tried to sear Roldin with his best glare. The man leaned back with a frown. "Well, you're *definitely* your mother's child."

Just then Penny opened the door, a bundle of bags in her arms, and smiled at her son. "Hey swee—what are you doing here?"

Roldin smiled as widely as he could, holding onto his crutch while trying to stand up and hobble over to her with some dignity. Before he could say anything Linder announced, "He said I'm a cheater."

"Did he, now?" she said and raised an eyebrow at the demon slayer, who laughed weakly.

"Oh, silly kids, you know," he said, turning to the boy and making a shushing motion. Linder stuck his tongue out.

Roldin turned back to the lady of the house. "Hello, good day, my lady barmaid. Uh, Penny. I just wanted to talk to you for a moment."

She put down her groceries and began sorting through the bags. "What could you possibly want to talk to me about, 'Blackthorn'?"

"That," he said, pointing at her, "that right there is why I need to talk to you, and soon." He reached out to take her arm but she shrugged him away and continued unpacking the bag.

Roldin sighed, leaned over, and began helping her, pulling a jar from the bag. She snatched it out of his hand with a glare and placed it on a shelf. "Excuse me," she said with a raised eyebrow. "I will be with you in a moment if you wait outside."

"But it's raining."

"There's an awning in the back," she said icily. Roldin obeyed immediately, not even stopping to retrieve his boots

For several minutes Roldin tried to fit all of himself under the awning, getting his bare feet soaked in the process. Penny finally marched out of the house and faced him with her apron held aloft to stave off the rain "All right, what is it you want?"

Roldin thanked her and smiled brightly, but the barmaid's steely gaze remained unwavering. The demon slayer cleared his throat and dropped his overly-friendly façade. "Yes, well, I wanted to talk to you about last night. About anything you may have overheard."

"Like what, Roldin?"

He jumped and put both arms out to shush her, also losing his crutch. Penny looked on with amusement as he tried to lean over without bending his left leg to retrieve it. "Listen, my name—my real name— is a very dangerous one. I would very much appreciate it if you didn't tell anyone what you heard last night."

She crossed her arms and regarded him for several long moments. "Blackthorn sounds insane," she said. "I liked Krill Tempest— the name you used when you came to Levin's Ferry— better."

He nodded, "Yes, yes, well I had to retire that name, too," he said, then paused. "Wait, you really think that's better than Gaeryn Blackthorn? I spent a week coming up with Blackthorn!"

"It sounds like something out of a bad book."

"Yeah, I know, I probably read that book when I was a child, and three of its sequels." He shrugged and shook his head. "It's theatrical. People love it!"

"Apparently they do, but it's like something you would find scribbled on a thirteen-year-old boy's bedroom wall, along with drawings of swords and busty women."

Roldin bristled. "You said you liked Krill Tempest, and that was one of my worst ones, probably ever. I mean, I have to say it makes me really question your taste when you were younger."

"With the things I did when I was eighteen," Penny replied venomously through narrowed eyes, "yes, I'd say I had questionable taste, indeed."

The demon slayer wrinkled his nose then nodded slowly. "Well done."

Penny dipped a small curtsy. Her face turned serious. "Listen, I know what I heard last night, but more importantly, I know what I saw. That demon was not after her; it was after you. And you led it here and put this whole town in danger!"

"I—all right," he nodded and shrugged. "It's true; it was after me. At least I gave the town a warning and got everyone to safety first so I could take care of it. What's the harm if I wanted a dry place to sleep and maybe a few drinks first?"

"And have the town pay you for being a hero?"

"That's just a nice little bonus. Besides, I did kill a demon and save the town, right? You were there and you saw what happened."

"Except, if you weren't here, it wouldn't have come to town, now would it?"

"That's not necessarily true," he said, raising a finger. "It very well could have happened upon this town to feed and kill everyone here just so it could chase me a little longer. I just beat it to the punch."

Penny sighed and thought for a moment. "Is that why your name is dangerous?"

"Yes. A whole cadre of demons is after me," Roldin began ticking off a list on his fingers. "The cultists who worship them are after me, the cultist's dogs and second-cousins and barbers are after me—not to mention the entire kingdom of Adren."

"You're in Adren, you know."

Roldin looked up sharply. "What? Since when?"

"We were annexed two years ago. King Twill took the whole county as part of the 'new kingdom of peace' he claims he's building to unite the land. A lot of people at the county seat were killed. It's not been so bad, so far, out here. Road's End just does what we're told. Why does Adren want you? Did you try to sleep with Twill's daughter or something?"

"It's a long story," he said, leaning around the corner of the house and looking around the town with new eyes. There were no guards in sight, but now he was more worried about what he couldn't see. "I need to get out of here."

"Finally, we agree on something."

"Very funny," Roldin said, then leaned heavily on his crutch. "Have to heal up a little first. Hopefully things will stay quiet." He sighed, looked over at Penny, then through the window at Linder. "Despite what you think of me, I don't like putting anyone in danger." The barmaid rolled her eyes and looked away. Roldin scratched the back of his head. "He seems like quite a smart boy."

She looked back into the house with a smile, where Linder sat engrossed in his book. "He's something, isn't he? Such a wise little man. Too wise for his own good, sometimes."

"Where's his father?"

"That is none of your business," she said with hard eyes. "I'm not going to spread your name around, if that's what you're worried about, so you can go."

He bowed quickly. "Thank you. I promise I'll be out of town as soon as I can."

She nodded. The demon slayer went back into the house to collect his belongings. Linder looked up from his book. "I'll try to read it like I'm supposed to, like you said."

Roldin smiled, unaware of Penny looking at the man with surprise. "Good. It's a good story."

"Worth eating?"

"I—yes, it's certainly worth eating," he laughed. "It was nice to meet you, Linder." Roldin felt the smile on his face even as he hobbled back into the rain.

Chapter 3

Three Coins and a Halfer

The rain did nothing to dampen the spirits of the revelers. The citizens of Road's End always prided themselves on being practical folk: they wasted nothing, they kept excessive use of supplies to a minimum in case of catastrophe, and they did not open themselves up to risks of any kind. But this party was held precisely because catastrophe was averted. Plus, the spring rains had been long, the previous winter even longer, and they had over a season's worth of inactivity to shake off. So the residents spared no expense.

A sluice gate was set up at the end of the town's three spring rivers, and all day children went about creating boats out of wood, parchment, paper, and whatever else they could find. The town candlewaxer worked overtime and gave each child a candle the color of gold. As the sun set and the rains slowed for just an instant, a dozen children launched a dozen boats with a single candle in each one, and the makeshift crafts worked their way down the flooded waterways, illuminating the water like fallen stars. The townspeople watched with delight as the boats made their way through the canals, dancing in currents here and there, passing under houses and plankways, and finally ending up trapped against the gate at the end. Here, the small ships promptly caught fire against each other and went down in a blaze of glory, which all the children enjoyed with amazement, whoops, and hollers.

Inside the tavern, flagons of mead, beer, and whiskey —even Kinnley's finest wine — flowed generously for cooped-up citizens. One of the miners, his moustache the color of charcoal and his eyes rheumy and red, surprised all his friends by taking up the flute again and playing a lively tune. Another of the miners kept rhythm on a small drum. Only the most observant of citizens noticed the constant sneers each gave the other, as the two men never played in time together the whole evening. Most of the townsfolk didn't care—they just wanted the sound of music to carry them away.

Gaeryn Blackthorn, guest of honor, sat at the end of a long table that was set up in the middle of the common room. Next to him sat the mayor, with Constable Jodas seated nearby as well. After him came the head of the mine, a skinny man with a permanent frown who would have rather been counting his coins. Clariya and her family were seated down at the end. Roldin danced once with Clariya, then took the girl's mother out for a polite two-step, then her nine year old sister, who kept trying to kiss him. A couple of the older village girls took him aside and giggled as they tried to teach the demon slayer a complicated line dance, but his crutch prevented him from doing anything too intricate. Roldin had to admit the crutch was a much better excuse than the usual one he gave whenever dancing came up: he had two left feet.

Old man Silas came around to pat him on the back. "Well done there, sir," he said, shaking Roldin's hand in a strong grip. "Would be, if I were younger, I could've helped you out last night, you know. I could swing a mean pick axe in my younger days."

The demon slayer bowed. "I'll remember that next time, if there is one." Silas beamed and excused himself to go back to the bar, where he boasted about how he would have helped Blackthorn fell that demon in a moment if he were just a year or two younger. Wull shook his head with a smile as he poured the old man a shot of whiskey, and Penny practically threw a small trencher of bread and stew at him, telling him to stop talking nonsense.

There were toasts, as well— many toasts, by many people, with many excuses to drink. Soon the entirety of the tavern was in good spirits and shook the floor with dancing and laughing and contests of daring. A couple of the men threw horseshoes in a corner that was worn by hundreds of dents and scuffs from plenty of bad throws over the years. A few of the tougher miners took turns arm wrestling and taunting each other. Two old women—one of them Old Nanny, Roldin was surprised to see — challenged each other to a knife throwing competition. Even though both had to squint to see their target, once they made it out they never missed. The medicine woman's husband declared this was why he didn't step out on his wife. He barely ducked as a knife whizzed over his head.

Roldin couldn't help but enjoy himself. The mayor quietly passed him a bag full of coin under the table during the party, along with another set of thanks. From the weight of the bag it was a substantial sum, and the demon slayer had the grace to be slightly ashamed of himself. That lasted only for a few moments before a maiden leaned over to him and planted a quick kiss on his mouth before running away giggling.

The town's shopkeeper raised his glass in a toast and began thanking everyone who ever did anything nice for him, breaking down at one point over the happiness he felt over being alive. This caused a new round of merriment and laughing and crying in the tavern. The noise of the moment was deafening, and, with a laugh, Roldin got up and excused himself from the table. He approached the bar and asked Penny for a mug of mead.

She put it down in front of him, leaning toward him slightly. The demon slayer did likewise, so he could hear as she smirked and said, "Three coins and a halfer for the savior of Road's End." Roldin held her gaze with a smirk of his own as he counted out the coins on the bar with slaps of his palm and slid them over to her.

With his mug in one hand and his crutch in the other, the demon slayer made his way out the tavern door and stood on the covered porch, breathing deep of the damp night air. The town stretched out before him, darker than usual as everyone was here, celebrating. Roldin looked back inside and saw people laughing and joking with friends. They probably hadn't realized he had gone.

He drank the mead, savoring it, enjoying a moment of peace. As he took a final deep swig, finishing it off, he thought he saw movement across the other walkway. It was only for an instant, a darker shape amongst the darkness, but it was there, and it was moving fast—faster than any normal person would be travelling in the dead of night. Normally he would use his ears as well as his eyes to detect things in the deep woods when he was cornered, but the sound of merriment was too deafening behind him. He set his mug down on the railing and started shuffling down the plankways as fast as his crutch could carry him.

The sounds from the tavern eventually quieted. He could hear the rain dropping lightly but persistently into the water. The flooded road waters rushed below him. An owl hooted from the forest nearby. Footsteps to his left. He turned and walked forward, cursing his injured leg and the clumsy crutch that carried him. His right hand reached for his axe as he saw a dark figure materialize before him.

A short body almost barreled into him with a yelp. Roldin reached out and grabbed a skinny arm, then loosened his grip suddenly. "Linder?"

The boy gasped but gradually recognized him. "Oh, hi, Gaeryn," he said.

"Linder, what are you doing out here?" Roldin asked, exasperated. "It's...it's probably not safe for you. It's dark out."

"I'm looking for Ma," he said.

"You should go home. Here, let me take you," Roldin said, and he put a hand on the boy's back to turn him around.

"But I need to tell Ma about the strangers."

Roldin stopped fast. "What strangers?"

"Across from the house. I keep seeing people out there, but no one's lived in the Crawsons' place all year." Roldin gripped the boy's shoulder protectively and looked around. He could see nothing.

"Let's take you home and then I'll take a look, all right?"

Linder nodded. Roldin took the boy's hand and the two walked slowly and quietly through the dark wooden plankways of Road's End. Between Roldin's crutch and the inky blackness they made poor time, but Linder seemed to know his way around and guided them well. "I'm almost done with the book," he confessed quietly. "I think it may have a sad ending, though."

Roldin absently squeezed the child's hand as he strained to see anything around them. "Don't worry about that."

They arrived at the walkway to Penny's house and Roldin leaned over as best he could to get to eye level with the boy. "Linder, I need you to go home and don't come out. Lock the door, put out your candles, and don't open the door for anyone, do you understand?"

Linder nodded seriously. "I can do that."

"Is this the house, the Crawsons'?" Roldin asked the boy, pointing to a dark shack on the main road. Linder nodded. "Thank you. And remember, lock the door."

Roldin waited until the boy was in the house. He could hear the click of a lock sliding into place, and the windows went dark. The slayer turned, surveying the vacant house where Linder had seen strangers. He could see nothing at all. He made his way down the walkway nearest to it, reaching for a door with his hand. He felt it and pushed it open easily. The inside was just as dark as the outside.

He stepped in anyway, out of the rain. The floor creaked under his weight, and, looking down at it, he could just make out many waterlogged footsteps passing through the house ahead of him. Roldin closed the door, wincing against the creaking sound, and stooped down to remove his boots. Barefoot, he shuffled as quietly as he could through the house, bumping into stacked and stored furniture here and there. He fought the urge to use his crutch and was simply easy on his wounded leg instead, afraid he would make more noise.

The demon slayer began to hear voices. From what little light that came in through the shuttered window nearest him he could see the puddles of water end abruptly. Squinting, he could make out a trap door, which he struggled to bend down and open as quietly as possible.

Candlelight flickered at him from below, and he could now make out a rhythmic chanting. Roldin knew that sound all too well and the hair on the back of his neck stood on end. As dangerous as demons were, Roldin usually admitted that human cultists filled him with more ire. It was man who called demons to the world once upon a time, and it was man who continued to do so even now.

Evil men — men like his father — and men who wished to dabble in darkness.

Quickly and quietly, ignoring the searing pain that shot through his leg with every step he took down the narrow staircase into the basement, he descended. He took the last two steps into the cold water flooding the floor and licking up at his shins. He could see light and shadows around a corner. Drawing his axe and ignoring the sounds he made as he trudged through the water, he rounded the bend.

There were five men. Two were seated on tables cross-legged, and they had already cut their forearms to let their blood drip onto the heartstone shards set out before them, and were lost in a deep trance. The other three had rolled their sleeves and were about to do the same. These three turned as he came into view.

"It's him," the tallest of them growled. Roldin could see a tattoo on the man's bare arm that bore the jagged symbol of the largest cult of demon worshippers.

"He's wounded," the bald one laughed, eyeing his crutch.

"Your lucky day," Roldin said with a snarl as he lifted his axe with his right arm and leaned on his crutch with the left, "don't try to be gentle."

The one nearest him, shorter with a thick head of dark shaggy hair, charged, his ritualistic dagger held aloft. Roldin shifted his weight on his right leg, twirled his crutch around in his left hand, grabbed the end of it, and used it to knock aside the dagger thrust. Roldin's right arm swung around and buried the axe in the man's chest so hard that his feet left the ground before he fell face-first into the flood waters.

Baldy and the big man advanced. Leaving his axe in the fallen cultist, Roldin held his crutch before him like a staff. As the bald man feinted halting thrusts with his dagger the taller man edged behind Roldin in a flanking position. Roldin abruptly twisted and drove the crutch into the gut of the cultist behind him, taking the wind out of him and bending the tall man in half. Thinking he saw an opening, the clean-shaven cultist lunged. The demon slayer turned and caught the man's wrist with his hand, twisted once with a hard well-practiced jerk, and broke the cultist's wrist. As the man's ritual dagger fell, Roldin tipped and caught the handle in midair, grunting as he accidentally put too much pressure on his left leg. He flipped the dagger grasping it by the blade and flung it. In a practiced arch that would have rivaled the medicine woman's, Roldin's throw hit one of the two cultists who were deep in summoning, burying deep in the side of the man's neck. His chanting stopped.

While the bald-headed man held his broken wrist and howled, the tall man recovered, grabbing Roldin from behind. The demon slayer was forced to drop his crutch as the larger man brought a dagger around and tried to bury it in his chest. Roldin struggled to hold back the dagger with his right arm and the cultist managed a shallow gash at his shoulder. The metal of the dagger was unusually cool against his skin, and the wound was already growing cold and numb. As he struggled, the demon slayer could make out intricate patterns on the blade's surface and the metal itself was a dark green color that could not have been made naturally. It was obviously conjured, a gift from a demon to a loyal servant.

With his left hand the demon slayer grabbed his attacker's right arm. Roldin shifted all his weight to his own left leg, causing it to buckle, and he used that sudden momentum to flip the tall man overhead and square onto his back, landing the cultist's head underwater. Roldin wrenched the dagger from his attacker's hand and stabbed the cultist with two precise strikes, once in the neck and again between his ribs, nicking his heart.

Roldin stood, hopped over to the last remaining summoner, and knocked the heartstone off of the table and onto the floor just as the shadows around it began to strengthen. Water washed the blood from the stone and the summoning was rendered inert. The man opened his eyes at the sound— the last thing he saw was a dagger lunging towards his left eye.

The demon slayer looked at the dagger in his hand with disgust. Just holding it was causing his skin to crawl; it made his already numb fingers worse. He buried the dagger deep in the wood of the tabletop, took hold of the grip with both hands, and wrenched as hard as he could against the flat of the blade. The weapon was snapped in two, and the blade and hilt pieces dissipated in a plume of dark green smoke.

The bald man with the badly broken wrist shakily stood and saw that all of his cohorts were dead. Roldin hobbled back toward him, turned the shaggy-haired body of his fellow cultist over, and wrenched the dark bladed axe free. The demon slayer limped through the bloody waters towards his final foe.

"It doesn't matter now, Benirus," the man taunted with manic, laughing sobs. His eyes were bloodshot and wide. "You're dead! The demons have other plans for you now, oh yes."

Roldin paused. "What plans? Start talking sense."

The cultist's laughing intensified as he was backed against the basement wall. "You'll never stop us!" the bald man said with a frenzied shout. "All shall perish as the demons cleanse this sinful world of the living and make it anew! We are not worthy to live in their —"

The demon slayer silenced the ranting with a single strike of his axe. "When will they figure out what side they're on?" Roldin muttered with a heavy shake of his head. He sighed deeply, let out a cough, and found his crutch in the water. He shook it off and leaned heavily on it. Taking one of the candles around the room and holding it aloft, he illuminated the grisly sight and began to search the bodies. On each corpse he found a parchment with the name of a demon, and he gathered them all together laying them out on one of the recently abdicated tables.

The list of names was not what he expected. Yunirax was the only name he recognized. The demon slayer stared at the parchments for a long time, mulling over the cultist's final words. Something new was happening and he was not privy to it, yet, which did not put his mind at ease at all. He had grown accustomed to being one step ahead of his foes; it was necessary for survival.

Roldin pocketed the parchments as well as every heartstone shard he could find. He made his way back up the stairs to the main floor and shut the trapdoor, sliding a piece of furniture over top. He'd have to deal with the bodies later. He stepped out into the rain-soaked night. Through the regular evening sounds he could make out the celebration still going on in the tavern. He looked down at himself, covered in blood, water, and worse — not exactly party attire. Roldin leaned against his crutch and began to weigh his options.

#

A couple of hours later Penny rushed through the rain back home, her apron over her head. She came to a stop as she noticed that her usually well-lit house was very dark. She was preparing herself for the worst when a shape near her front door moved. The barmaid jumped.

"Roldin?" she asked, able to make out the demon

slayer sitting against her house, axe and crutch crossed before him. He was covered in blood. "Is—"

"He's fine," he said quickly. "Sleeping. I wanted to watch the house until you came back."

She looked at the blood. "Was there another demon here?"

"No. Cultists," he spat. "They won't be a problem anymore."

"You're wounded," she said, looking at the gash in his shoulder.

"It'll heal. I have more pressing problems," he said. "I've put this town in more danger than I realized. Word that I'm here has spread quickly. I need to get away, now. Do you have a boat I can borrow to get through the flood lands?"

"I can get you a skiff," she said, then put her hands on her hips. "Where do you expect you're going to go? There's not a town for miles and the flooding isn't deep enough for a boat for very far, so you'll have to walk after a mile or so out. You won't be moving fast with that leg."

"Anywhere," he said, and rubbed his face with his hands. "Though if I could find someone willing to summon a demon for me, that would be best."

Penny stared at him. "A demon slayer wants to summon a demon?"

"It's a long—"

"Story, yes, you have lots of those," she sighed. "I may actually know someone who could help you."

"Really? Where?"

"She..." she began, then Penny shook her head. "It's a long story." Roldin shot her a sardonic glance. "I'll just have to take you," she finished with a sigh.

CHAPTER 4

WORTHY OF A SAGA

By the time dawn crept across the sky, Penny and Roldin were in a skiff and rowing their way through the flooded forest at the base of Mount Everdare.

She had left Linder in the care of Wull, waking the boy quietly to let him know that she would be back soon. His only question was whether Gaeryn was safe and if he had taken care of the strangers. Linder sleepily added that he hoped so, that he liked Gaeryn. Penny was glad the boy had fallen back to sleep and hadn't seen the look on her face.

Penny pulled herself back to the present. "I'm taking you to a woman named Alys," she explained as they navigated downed trees and precarious bends. "She's from the university in Eganstown. A scholar — or maybe a student scholar, I'm not exactly sure. She came through Road's End last summer in search of some ruins out here that she's been studying. I've visited her a few times to give her provisions and check on her, made sure she survived the winter. She's hardy and stubborn, and I think she's a little mad. You'll like her."

"Oh, why wouldn't I?" Roldin asked. "Sounds delightful." The demon slayer guided the skiff around a ruined, moss-covered stone statue jutting out from the center of a flooded stand of trees. A gaping maw with rows of teeth stared back at him. On either side of the face, wings and claws had been formed in stone but they had long since worn down to nubs. He judged it to be centuries old. "This mountain has a lot of history. What kind of ruins does our scholar make her home in?" he asked.

"They belonged to some kind of demon cult, about three hundred years ago," she said. "That's all Alys told me."

"This keeps getting better," he muttered, "a demon scholar." Roldin continued to appraise the demon statue as their skiff rounded a bend and the effigy disappeared from sight. He wondered if anyone knew the name of the demon it was supposed to be the likeness of. "I suppose this is why you think she could help me summon a demon?"

"She seems very interested in the subject. But, she's a sweet girl. I trust her."

Roldin nodded. "Very well. I'll trust your judgment."

"Do you have a choice?"

"Don't start."

The rain continued to pelt them as they beached the skiff close to the slope of the mountain range. "We have to walk the rest of the way," Penny explained. "We should be there by mid-afternoon."

Roldin tapped his leg. "Sounds like a challenge, but I'll try my best."

The barmaid adjusted her pack and cloak around her shoulders and squinted as a burst of wind blew rain into her eyes. The showers couldn't completely conceal her sardonic smile. "He slays demons for a living, but a little morning walk is worthy of a saga."

"You try getting stabbed in the leg by a demon and see how fast you go," Roldin grumbled.

She didn't press the issue, and the two of them circled the base of the mountain range. "There's a path somewhere over here that leads up the mountain. It's old, if the remains of stone pillars around it are any hint. It's an easy hike — we don't need equipment to make it."

"I guess you know where you're going," Roldin said, though she could barely hear him above the rising sound of the howling winds. The trees above them swayed dangerously in gales that hit the mountain like a battering ram. The demon slayer was just glad that he wasn't trudging through flood waters anymore.

Roldin kept his eyes forward and looked for any trace of the forest trail. When Penny pointed, though it was faint, he could see the signs clearly enough. It looked like a path taken by traders and ore carts during the warmer months, but now it was ill-used and in danger of becoming overgrown. The green leaves of early spring were thick and wet under his feet.

He studied the back of the barmaid's head as she led the way. Ever since she'd claimed to know him he'd been struggling to remember her, but for some reason his mind was too hazy to recall their tryst. Roldin didn't doubt that it had happened, but those years of his life had been particularly hard, and a lot of that time was lost amid a golden haze of drink. Every so often, when she looked his way, before her signature grimace overtook her face, he thought he saw something there that was familiar. Then her scowl would erase any of that.

A particularly strong gust of wind halted their advance entirely. Roldin shielded his eyes from the piercing rain that came with it, realizing with a start that he couldn't see the trail ahead anymore — and Penny was a dull shape in the grey expanse. The wind and rain gave birth to a sudden storm, and the rumble of thunder that belched from the swirling clouds sent a tremor into the mountain above them.

"We have to get to some shelter!" he called out to her. Roldin could barely make out the woman nodding.

Her voice shook. "There's a cave not too far from here," she said, and motioned him to follow.

The rain, which had been a constant but bearable nuisance all morning, now struck them both like hammers. Penny struggled against the wind but Roldin fought his leg almost as much. His slower gait made him lose ground behind her. Though she kept turning to ensure he was following, soon enough he looked up and could no longer see the barmaid ahead of him.

"Penny!" he called out. The only response was the howling of the storm. He tried to determine where she had been going but his bearings were completely lost. Another thunderclap — accompanied by a flash of lightning that tore across his vision and struck a tree not too far from him — shook him to his core.

Roldin knew he was not safe in the open. He picked a direction and took off running, cursing his wounded leg. His breath already came in ragged gasps from the exertion of limping, and the stab of pain in his thigh told him he was doing his injury no favors, either. The pain got worse with each step as his vision became clouded further with flashes of light — not caused by the lightning storm around him, but his whole body's revolt against his predicament. Roldin winced through the pain, fought back the panic that threatened to engulf him, and kept moving. "One foot in front of the other," he told himself through gritted teeth, even as one of those feet failed to obey.

The experience of running for his life proved to feel awfully familiar. Aside from the sensory bombardment of rain, pain, fear, and wind, the years of being on the run had worn him down. That same desperation still clung to what he still possessed of his soul like a heavy, wet cloak. Roldin ran as deftly as he could muster considering his injury, blinded by the storm around him. He heard a voice on the wind — faint, but there. The demon slayer turned and advanced on it, feeling his way through trees and rocks and battering wind.

A large dark shape loomed before him, and he could clearly hear Penny calling his name. He stumbled forward into the cave, the sudden absence of rain and wind instantly disorienting him. She helped him drag himself further inside, away from the storm's wrath, and, together, they collapsed in two breathless heaps.

"Thought I'd lost you out there," she said between gasps.

"Me, too," he said, shaking his panic from his mind like a dog does water from his coat.

They crawled back into the cave as far as they could go. Roldin found enough dry kindling to start a small fire and the two of them tried their best to get warm. Penny shrugged off her pack and began to remove her clothes. Squeezing them free of rain water, she placed them on the dry floor of the cave behind her. The man tried his best to avoid the sight of her in her shift. "You've seen me naked before, you know. I'd rather be shamed than dead from a chill," she chided him with a smirk.

"I suppose so," he said with a shrug, then worked on doing the same. The wind found its way inside the cave from time to time, bringing a dangerous cold right along with it. Roldin peeled off his armor and gingerly took off his shirt underneath. He buried his hands in his armpits and fought against his own shivers. Even with his arms crossed in front of him, an impressive track of scars was clearly visible on his skin, including the fresh wounds on his shoulder and forehead.

Penny watched the firelight dance off the shiny marks on his body. "You don't give up without a fight, do you?" she asked, trying as best she could to stop trembling.

"Not in my nature," he said with his best grin. The mirth did not meet his eyes. His gaze was far away.

Penny took some dried meat from her pack and handed it to the demon slayer. "I intended to give this to Alys, but I think she'd understand."

"Thank you," he said with a nod. He chewed on the meat without tasting it. The storm continued to rage outside, though the silence in the cave threatened to deafen it. "So, Road's End seems like a nice place."

"No it doesn't," Penny replied, narrowing her eyes. "It's a hopeless town at the end of civilization." She shrugged. "But it's home, I guess."

"Why stay?"

"Why not?" she countered. "It's a place to be, even with the deadly winters and endless spring floods. People are friendly enough. We have to be, since we're all in this thing together, I suppose." The barmaid rubbed her bare feet with her hands and tried to work warmth back into them. "You don't have a place to call home?"

Roldin opened his mouth a few times, then shook his head with a tight smile. "Never have. Father was a traveling merchant, so I've always been on the road, ever since I was little."

"What about your mother?"

"Died when I was too young to remember her. My father…did his best."

"You don't want to try settling down? Stop chasing

after demons? Maybe take a break from entrapping pretty young girls into spending the night with you?" There was a grin on her face, but Roldin couldn't tell if it was playful or judgmental.

He rolled his eyes. "I wouldn't have slept with her, you know."

"Oh, I'm sure your intentions were completely pure."

"I'm too old for that now, anyway, and for her especially," he said, running his fingers through his hair and shaking off the water. "But people always expect you to protect the pretty young maiden. Makes for a better story."

"And better tips?"

"Killing demons doesn't make for a very profitable living — unless you get creative." Roldin shrunk only a little bit under her steely-eyed glare. "But to answer your question, no, settling down has never really been in the cards. Also not in my nature. No one's in it with me."

"Oh, don't be overdramatic," she grumbled.

"I can't stay in one place for too long," he continued, shrugging off her accusatory stare. "Makes me nervous."

"Does being here make you nervous?"

"More than you could imagine."

She laughed. "The great Krill Tempest is scared of a drowned rat like me?"

"Not you," he said with a glare of his own. "This cave. Being stuck, being still. It…doesn't agree with me."

Penny raised an eyebrow and nodded. "So you long for the open road— the wind in your hair and society at your back, like some kind of vagabond hero?"

"You said it, not me," he laughed, and grinned

wolfishly at her displeased expression. "Though it's far less dramatic than that. I just keep moving. No decent place would take me in, anyhow. I'm not very comfortable around people."

Penny took her braid from over her shoulder and fiddled with it thoughtfully. "I have a cousin over in Neppeth. He has a shack in the poorer part of town, along some dusty road the city never bothered paving. Neighborhood's all thieves and cutthroats, most like, but he said no one ever looks anyone else in the eyes. He's never felt more alone among so many people."

Roldin shuddered. "I hate Neppeth," he said and spat in the fire.

"Beggars can't be choosers," Penny said with a low chuckle. "Have you ever even tried to settle down?"

"Of course I tried," he grunted, unfazed by her taunting glare. Roldin held his hands out above the smoldering fire and scrunched his nose. "Once. It was far to the east, about a dozen years back. It was on the coast, miles away from anything else. Remote." A ghost of a smile played on his lips and his voice softened. "I spent a month in a tiny fishing village. Found a pretty girl. We talked of marriage in the wee hours, cuddling together in blankets to stave off the midnight chill. I ended up being a pretty good fisherman, if I may say so myself. I liked it. It was quiet." He picked up a handful of kindling and tossed it on the fire. It flared to life, only briefly. "Peaceful."

"Why didn't you stay?" Penny asked softly.

The demon slayer's smile dropped from his face. "They found…" he cleared his throat, wiped his eye and quickly shook his head. "Let's just say that death has a habit of following me, and leave it at that. Wouldn't know what to do with quiet if I found it, anyway. I don't deserve it." Roldin pulled his hands close to his chest and cracked his knuckles. "I left the town behind and took to the road — like I was always meant to do."

"It can't be that bad. Sounds like you just take after your father. You —" Her voice caught in her throat — arrested by the sudden, dark, and dangerous look that crossed his face as swiftly as a storm cloud. Penny quickly put a piece of meat in her mouth and chewed slowly, afraid to meet the demon slayer's eyes.

#

The storm lasted the rest of the day. The already cloud-darkened sky turned gloomier as night took over. They ate more of the dried meet, collected water from the storm, and had minimal conversation. Their clothes having dried near the fire, they dressed again and Penny retreated to the back of the cave to begin mending her shoes. Roldin took up his axe in one hand and his crutch in the other, perching himself at the mouth of the cave.

"There's nothing to see out there," she called to him. The storm still raged without, shielding the whole mountain in a curtain of rain and howling wind.

"There's always something to see," he replied, softly so she could not hear him. His fingers danced on the dark axe in his grip, the wood worn smooth from years of use, taking comfort in its familiar weight in his hand. He scanned the murky dark, anyway, searching for threats in the night. Though it made no sense to Penny, the forbidding finality of the small cave that ended in a wall of stone behind him made his neck shiver more than the expansive, dark unknown that stretched out before him.

Penny stoked the fire and bundled up in her cloak to sleep, not saying anything to Roldin as she did so. Only moments later, he could hear her breathing slow to a steady pulse, with the barest hint of a snore on the edges. The demon slayer looked back at her, and in the warm glow of the fire that illuminated her still and frown-free face he suddenly remembered her: younger, happier, and laughing at his jokes and tales of daring near a fire in a tavern, years before. She had been scared, which was his fault, but she had also been full of life, and as feisty then as she was now. She'd matched his stories of bravado with jokes of her own.

He shook his head. Fate was an odd thing, bringing him back to someone he had known before. Roldin could say — with some certainty — that there were very few people he'd ever seen more than once. It was a consequence of his life, but it made things easier.

The demon slayer returned his attention to the storm. A lightning bolt shocked the sky awake and lit the forest for a sharp moment. Hundreds of claw-like tree limbs seemed to reach for him all at once in the flash of light, and the afterimage played with a mind that was already on edge. The grip on his axe tightened; his knuckles turned white.

The darkness called to him above the din of the storm with silent taunts out of nightmares, peering at him from its home amongst the unknown blackness that lay at the edge of every person's soul. The demon slayer stared it down glare for glare, with a useless axe in his hand — the only monster he could never truly slay.

Thirty Two Years Earlier

The boy had done as his father suggested; he ran. With only the cloak on his back and his father's dagger tucked in his belt, Roldin barely had anything to his name. What he did have was an uncomfortable sense that something was behind him. The feeling helped him keep running, despite his weariness, despite his fear, and despite his confusion about what had happened.

Hunger gnawed at him around the edges of his panic. He felt weak, but he had the impression that food would not help fill this emptiness. His chest still hurt where the creature had touched him. He felt drained, unnaturally so. The spot on his left palm still ached, and the drying blood remained sticky.

He walked down the side of the muddy road, suddenly missing that cart — even the barrel that always dug into his shoulder. His shoes were old and poorly made, and he was already beginning to outgrow them. Soon, his feet ached along with the rest of him. At least the rain had stopped.

The first town he approached was a farming village made up of a few buildings — most falling down — and a handful of people. He saw a family sitting on their stoop, just watching the road. They regarded him silently as Roldin passed them by. The boy wondered how he appeared — crazed and sick, most likely. He fought an urge to stop and ask them for food or help. He dared not go near anyone. Not yet.

He walked on. At one point he dashed into a corn field, taking a few ears from the stalks, evading working farmhands. Roldin ran away down the road out of sight before stopping to peel back the silks and eat it raw. He'd never stolen anything before. As he bit the sweet, crisp kernels from the cob, he figured the farmer wouldn't be missing a couple of ears.

The food did its job, but still he felt weak. The ends of his fingers and toes would go numb from time to time as he continued his walk "that way." Soon enough, he left the farmland and the road led him back into dense forest. He didn't like how dark it was.

As night fell, he stopped to rest under a rock set into a hill off the side of the road. He drank from a puddle of the day's rains, but had nothing else to eat. Roldin was accustomed to going a whole day on only one meal, and though he had devoured the pilfered corn a few hours before, he felt as if there was a hole inside him that he couldn't appease. His hands shook. Somehow sleep found him under the rock, whisking him away into a nightmare.

#

He was in a room without light, laying on a table, unable to move, but not bound by anything he could see. He was naked. As he looked down, his body looked impossibly thin and shriveled. His skin was stretched taught over jutting bones. There was a pulsating spot where his heart should be. He thought he could see blood rushing through thick veins, fighting to keep him alive.

Red eyes, seven pair in all, watched him from the shadows. He closed his eyes against their ravenous stares. He could feel movement around him. Hairs on his body stood on end, alert to an unseen force that hovered around the edges of his being.

"We've found you..." a feminine voice said, inches from his ear.

#

The boy woke in the middle of the night to a ringing in his ears and the echo of the voice in his head. Something on the back of his neck told him to move. Now. He rose, sobbing lightly from the sudden exertion and inexplicable fear. As he slipped from his hiding place, wild animal sounds he didn't recognize encircled him and he jumped at every single one. He frequently looked behind himself as he ran, never seeing anything, but feeling something stalking him in the darkness.

Roldin kept moving until he found a cabin off the road, deeper into the woods. He could see smoke rising from the chimney, but the windows were dark – the family inside lay asleep. With the unseen fear following him, he crept over to the house as quickly as he dared and found an open window. He crawled inside and found himself in a kitchen that was warmed slightly by the dying embers of the fireplace.

Food was not his primary concern at the moment. The fear that had followed him was ringing in his ears with a silent scream of warning. He saw an open space between a cupboard and a wall and squeezed himself inside. Roldin hid.

Nothing happened.

The only sounds he could hear were his labored breathing and the swift beating of his heart. Both sounded unbelievably close in the tight space he had crawled into. Minutes went by; hours, probably. The boy had buried his head between his knees and held his hands behind his head, as if the position could ward off whatever had attacked him on the road. The rest of the house was quiet.

He was beginning to feel foolish – was wondering how he was going to get out of the kitchen without being seen – when he heard a creaking above him, from the roof. Roldin held his breath. He could hear other sounds nearby – sounds of the sleeping family stirring. He heard a man's voice ask a question, and a woman's voice answer. Two sets of smaller feet were stepping through the house as well, and he heard children's sleepy voices speak to one another.

The man asked another question, and then a sudden crash shook the house's foundations. Roldin heard wood splinter and fall. The man yelled out, then his voice was suddenly replaced by a gurgling sound. The woman screamed. Her children screamed. He heard the family run into another room of the house as something impossibly large lumbered slowly, but persistently, after them. The floorboards around Roldin trembled as the thing went by.

The fear in his head told him to run. With a silent scream of panic he craned his head out from his hiding place. Through the kitchen door he could see a man lying on the ground in the next room, his throat a wet, red ruin. Roldin could still hear the screams of the family as something chased them through the house. One of the children suddenly ran past the door. She was followed by something large and dark, with scales, and claws, and shimmering slime all over its body. It was a creature like what had attacked him on the road, but it was noticeably different, "other." In the terror of the moment, he couldn't say how he knew that, but he did.

He only saw it for an instant, but that was enough. After the creature trudged out of sight, Roldin ran for the open kitchen window, slipped outside, and fled into the night. The boy's feet carried him as fast as they could go. He left the screams and roars of the house behind him and he didn't stop. Roldin had the horrifying thought that he might not ever stop running again.

#

The boy found a road and followed it, heading toward the town of Neppeth. Three nights of the next seven, he was likewise sure that something was coming for him in the dark, and Roldin had leapt up from his hiding place, running until his feet gave out. He began to call that feeling the Dread.

The tears that coursed down his face every night as he waited for the Dread stopped after a few more days. The pain in his heart went numb, like his fingers and toes did sometimes. More than anything, he was scared and confused. Every once in a while he felt a flash of anger and found his father's dagger in his hand. He didn't remember unsheathing it, and he would look at it curiously.

He thought about stopping the few merchants he saw along the road and trading the dagger for some food or new clothes. The blade would certainly be worth enough to do so, as well as give him coin leftover to do whatever he wanted with; he was a peddler's son, after all, and knew how to haggle. If whatever was chasing him looked like what he had seen in the house, what use would a dagger be, anyway? Something told him, however, to keep it – other dangers awaited him on the road beside the things that came in the night.

When he finally reached Neppeth he paused before the great wooden gates, afraid to enter. It was a large town, though not as large as Adren had been. There was a steady stream of traffic going in and out, so he certainly would not attract attention if he entered. Still, he'd seen things in towns of that size that scared him. Young children had a habit of suddenly vanishing.

Instead, he spent the day walking the surrounding forest, watching the town warily. He found a comfortable place next to a stream to sleep. He ate berries, only making himself sick twice. Outside Neppeth, he had his first truly restful night's sleep in weeks. The next day he conjured up the courage to enter the town during the bright mid-morning. He saw it, not through the eyes of a peddler, but with the ingenuity of a hungry child, and he saw infinite possibilities.

Roldin eyed fruit stands and bread baskets and racks of meat cooking on open fires, all out for purchase. He passed by stalls with clothes and shoes for sale. It also became apparent to him that, as innocent as he looked, shopkeepers didn't care for children to hang about their stalls staring at things. It was obvious to him he would need to be quicker: find what he wanted, figure a way to snatch it, and vanish into the crowd.

His first day in town, he was mostly unsuccessful. His first priority was food. He had gone so far as to get a hand around a piece of bread before a merchant caught him, and he dashed off without his prize, right out of the city and back into the safety of the woods.

That night he mulled over staying there, next to his stream. The trees above him had sparse branches, and he had a good view of the sky and plenty of light during the day. There was a small mossy rock overhang he could sleep under for shelter from rain. The water was cool and refreshing. The chance for a place to sleep more than once was enticing to him.

Just as he was dozing off the Dread came back to him — the silent ringing scream in his ears — pulling him out of a deep sleep. Mechanically, he stood up and wrapped his cloak around himself, picked a direction, and ran. He ran for hours, until the woods were quiet, but not too quiet, and the Dread left the back of his neck and the inside of his head alone.

The next day he returned to the town, but not to the stream. He walked to the opposite side of the town, found a log to sit on, and settled in to think. He saw the town as a trap. If whatever was out there chasing him found him inside the walls, he would have nowhere to run.

For that reason he retreated every day to the forest just outside. He became quite good at finding places to sleep quickly, and making sure that he never boxed himself in trees or rocks so that he could run in whatever direction he wanted when he needed to.

He began to get the hang of theft. He wasn't proud of himself, but he was hungry. He took an apple here or a small meat pie there. Most importantly, he managed to pinch a pair of shoes that had been made for a boy about his size. He'd watched that morning, from an alley across the street, as the boy and his family visited the cobbler; watched as the cobbler worked all day, and waited for when the shoes were laid out. Then he rushed over and grabbed the pair and ran until he was outside the town.

They sort of fit; he had to mess with the ends with his dagger so his feet would be comfortable inside. He felt a little guilty about stealing from the boy, but the feeling of real padding beneath his feet — instead of a sole worn so thin that he could feel every rock on the ground — more than made up for that.

Roldin learned Neppeth's streets well. He figured out which shopkeepers were the laziest about keeping an eye out, which ones had the freshest bread and when, which ones had the guards, which ones would beat you if they caught you, and which ones would let you go with a half-hearted yell from their chairs. It was also nice for him to walk among people again and hear the conversations and rumors of the day. Apparently the war that had he'd remembered hearing was brewing was already over somehow. The Lord Twill of Adren had been the easy victor over his neighbor Parvia. As for how the tables had turned so quickly in his favor, no one knew. It was the most popular mystery he heard people discussing.

Other homeless children like him plied their thieving trade as well. He steered clear of them. Either they didn't mind him because he didn't make his home in the streets like they did or they just couldn't catch him, Roldin didn't know.

He stored any extra food and clothes he stole in an empty tree trunk, but he never slept there. Nightly, and sometimes during the day, too, the Dread would come, and he would run. He would return the next day and pick another site, always close to Neppeth's walls but never inside them. Soon he noticed that he was working his way in a circle slowly around the town. While his pattern was not ideal, it worked, but he would soon run out of options and have to move on. He preferred not to think about that. The thought of being out in the middle of the wilderness again — alone and away from any civilization at all — terrified him.

Worse than the chases, he had to admit, were the nightmares. At first, he wrote them off as the obvious side effect of a sleep-deprived, rattled mind. But, as the nights went by, the dreams kept coming, and the creatures in them changed, too. Sometimes the things behind the eyes would speak to him. Sometimes they would hurt him. Sometimes up to seven others were with him; other times just one. They had their own personalities and their own tricks to inflict their cruelty on him. Patterns emerged, and he began to realize the creatures were consistent. As tired as he was, he began to fear sleep. He could run from them while awake; he couldn't escape his own mind.

Occasionally that Dread was accompanied by feral sounds in the distance – snarls and howls of animals that didn't belong in the forest, that were not natural. Sometimes he would actually feel something right behind him, barreling through the woods, or whispering with the wind.

Once, he went into town and the only talk was about guards being murdered inside the walls, their throats ripped open, or being disemboweled and left hanging from the guard posts. Whatever killed the guards could have been anything, he told himself. It wasn't the things looking for him. He heard people whisper "maniacs," and then "demons," and the implications scared him too much to hear any more. Roldin didn't spend much time in the town that day.

He'd developed his own pattern, but still the fear was always with him, and it was beginning to wear him down. At night, when the Dread returned, his reactions were becoming sluggish. Part of him, buried deep inside, wanted to end the chase. But would that be his death, he wondered. Or would the six more coming for him do whatever the first one had done, leaving him alive but petrified and helpless?

He was eager for neither fate.

CHAPTER 5

AN OLD FRIEND

In the morning they left the forest behind entirely as the greater part of the storm passed them by, and continued up the mountain slope. It was thick with rocks and crags. Roldin could tell where they were headed as soon as they went a little way up the mountain, despite the constant trickle of rain in his eyes. A stone keep, obviously cut from the same rock as the mountain, sat gloomily ahead of them. One of the towers had fallen sometime over the last three centuries and half of it lay in pieces on its side. The keep would have made an imposing fortress once, Roldin reasoned, but now it really was a crumbling ruin in every sense.

"Alys!" Penny called out when they got near. "Alys, it's Penny!"

Roldin leaned against what used to be part of the tower and rubbed his leg. It was getting warmer, he thought, but it was hard to tell in the cold drizzle and combative wind. Their flight from the storm yesterday certainly had not helped it, and he had awoken feeling somehow more tired than when he had finally resigned himself to get some sleep. His thoughts were interrupted by a coughing fit that lasted longer than normal, leaving him winded. A bird flew overheard, large and dark, and voiced a complaint at the strangers making noise on its mountain. He looked back and thought he could make out

Road's End poking out among the trees in the flooded forest far below.

"Alys!" Penny called again.

Finally a nest of dark hair peeked over one of the ruined towers. "Penny!" a high voiced cried. "What are you doing here?"

"I have someone I want you to meet," Penny called out, "and we need your help."

"Someone wants my help? This has never happened before. Amazing!" Alys cried, and disappeared again.

Roldin gave Penny a look. The barmaid cleared her throat. "She's really sweet," she said.

A door opened nearby and a diminutive woman came out wearing simple trousers and a tunic, covered with dust and dirt. Her look came complete with a tool belt and sheaves of parchment sticking out of a bag slung across her shoulder. She was probably much younger than Penny, with large brown eyes stuck at the top of a round, olive-colored face, and a perpetually interested expression. Her black hair was a tall tangle of knots with ribbons tying it back haphazardly, and charcoal pencils and other writing instruments stuck in at all angles. She wore oversized spectacles that made her eyes look even bigger and the rest of her head smaller. She gave Penny a quick hug and studied the demon slayer with her head tilted to one side. "Who's your friend?"

"Alys this is…" Penny looked to him for guidance.

He felt no reason to lie now. "My name is Roldin, Roldin Benirus."

Her already oversized eyes seem to grow twice as large. "No…no it can't be…can it?" She walked right up to him, studying his armor and cloak. When she saw his dark-bladed axe on his hip she jumped. "That's real moon-iron isn't it? I've never seen any in person before! Oh, it really is! I mean, you really are! This is amazing!"

Penny looked at both of them, confused. "You've heard of him?"

"Oh by the Sacreds, of course!" she exclaimed, talking a mile a minute. "It's the boy with the seven souls. Everyone's heard that old story. This is so remarkable! I..." she paused and studied him more intently than ever, reached out a finger, and poked him – hard – in the shoulder.

"Ow," he said.

"Wow, you really are alive!" she laughed.

"You could have asked instead of just poking..." he grumbled.

"I thought you were dead! Well, not that I've heard anything for sure about you lately...how many demons are still after you now, anyway?"

"Five," Roldin said, rubbing his shoulder.

"Wow," she said, as she put her hands together and hopped again. "Well, come in, come in! Let me show you around! Are you hungry or thirsty? I can give you food and water. Especially you, Penny, since you bring me the food and water to begin with, so it would be kind of circular if I fed you your own things, wouldn't it? How odd!"

Penny leaned over to Roldin and quietly said, "She doesn't get out much."

She led them through the door and into a large antechamber that, at one point, would have been grand. Now the ceiling was caved in and most of the stone that was once elaborately carved was weathered and worn smooth by the wind and rain, though Roldin could still just barely make out similar engravings to the stone statue he'd seen in the flood waters. The faces were looking down on him, eyes dark in the shadows, from nooks built into the walls. Alys had laid out some carpets that made an easy trail to follow under parts of the ceiling that still served as shelter. "The fort was one of the first ones built in the twenty years after the first demons came," Alys explained excitedly. "There's a wealth of information here, with stone carvings everywhere in some of the better preserved parts of the keep. Oh, you should see the crypts! The stuff they were buried with will scare you silly!"

"I'll pass," Penny said gently.

Alys led them to a smaller chamber that was more intact than the rest. There was a handcart parked in the corner, and scattered all around the room were books of all kinds. They were stuffed in shelves and on top of stone stools and under plates and bowls. There were papers everywhere with rubbings and notes on a section of the floor that the scholar seemed to be using as a giant desk. The trio had to carefully sidestep parchments to get to the other end of the room.

Roldin crossed the space and started looking through one of the makeshift bookshelves. "This is quite a collection."

"Thank you," Alys said with a little bounce. "I never go anywhere without my books. It's honestly kind of a problem."

The demon slayer silently read off the titles one by one. "Ah," he suddenly said with a smile, and took a book from the shelf. "*The Pauper Prince and the Sword of Kuralee.* This was my favorite book when I was a child!" He thumbed through it. "Better condition than the copy I used to own. I always wondered what the cover was supposed to look like…"

Alys smiled. "That is a good one isn't it? Oh, oooh, when he fights the demon army and saves the kingdom from certain doom? That's my favorite part! If only that kind of thing happened in real life. I mean, no matter how skilled he was he couldn't defeat a whole army, that would be totally impractical," she muttered as she dug through her stores to find food and waterskins.

Roldin brushed his hand over the cover with a thin smile, memories flooding back to him. He very much felt ten years old again. "Though, Alys...this isn't exactly scholarly, is it? Why is it here among all of your work books?"

"Oh, these aren't all work books, silly. As I said, I never go anywhere without my books." She obviously had no more to say on the subject and stared at the demon slayer expectantly. Roldin could only nod and smile.

Alys haphazardly kicked several of the papers away with her foot and cleared a space for them to sit on the floor. She handed them a jar of fish, a loaf of bread and some water then nibbled slowly on some herself. She continued talking at length about the keep, going into detail about how the stonework didn't match other examples from the same period, and how her theory was that it was designed and built by the demons themselves for their followers. Every once in a while she would get up in the middle of a sentence and grab a near-empty parchment from the pile and start scribbling vigorously. Then she would stick her charcoal pencil back in her hair, concentrate on folding the parchment until she couldn't get it any smaller, and throw it over her shoulder.

"So, my professor told me that the best way to write my paper on ancient demon cults and their cultural and socioeconomic impact on the early Panelda era was to go far, far away from him and study the old ruins myself, so that's exactly what I did!" She pushed her spectacles further up her nose and they fell back down immediately, but she didn't seem to notice. "You should have seen the looks on their faces as I left. They were so happy and proud of me. I can't wait to get back there and show them all that I found. It's going to make Hiribaldin's book on early demonic society look like childish fantasy. You were apprenticed under Varcus the Slayer, weren't you?"

Roldin looked up in surprise at the shift in subject, a handful of fish in his mouth. "For a short time, yes."

"Oooh, what was he like? I read a book about him when I was a young student and he seemed like such a fascinating person! He saw so many lands and killed so many demons in his travels. It must have been so exciting learning under him!"

The demon slayer finished swallowing his bite of fish. "That book was mostly true, but still full of lies. He was kind of an ass, actually. The only reason he taught me was to keep me close because I sort of acted as a demon dowsing stick for him due to the nature of my soul mark. Until, that is, I grew a little older, and the clear ringing sound I had heard when demons were near went away. I still had other gut feelings to warn me but those were harder to interpret and I got them frequently wrong. Also, we figured out I had six demons after me instead of just one. After that, it wasn't worth it to Varcus to keep a demon magnet on him at all times, so he wished me luck and sent me on my way when I was thirteen."

"Oh, that's sad," Alys said. Roldin shrugged. "Oh, I'm so silly," she said with a laugh. "Here I am babbling and you said you needed my help!" She wiped crumbs off of her mouth and folded her hands in her lap. "So, what can I do for you?"

Penny looked over at Roldin, who seemed to weigh his options for a couple of moments. Finally he sighed. "I need you to summon a demon for me."

Alys' jaw dropped. "Really? I mean, I've never summoned one before! I've wanted to…kind of, I mean I know they're not exactly friendly and I don't really want to give my soul up or anything, but I've always wanted to see one up close! Though, I don't have a heartstone or a name or anything to promise it, so I wouldn't know what to do, exactly."

"I have a heartstone, and I have a specific demon I want to talk to and a promise it will answer to. It's…friendly. Mostly. It's friendly with me, and I trust it, so it won't attack you or Penny. I need to ask it some questions."

"That…" she took a deep breath and put her hand over her mouth to suppress her smile. "That would be amazing! I'll do it. No, no, no, I can't do it wearing this! I have to find my…no, not that one, the other one!" She jumped up and scrambled out of the room, rushing by a stack of papers so fast that they went scattering to the floor.

Penny shot Roldin a worried look. "What did you mean by 'mostly' friendly?"

Roldin thought for a moment and chose his words carefully. "People usually have a wrong impression of demons. Most think them unquestionably evil. Sure, they can do some bad things, but intent has to be taken into account. Most demons just want power, which they happen to be able to get by killing us. Most think that demons ultimately want to just slaughter all of us, and that is true for some. But each demon has its own personality, its own agenda, and they also fight amongst themselves as to how our world is to be treated. The demon I want to summon, Saeralyx, is more interested in green fields and sunsets than with murder and mayhem."

"A good demon, huh?" Penny asked with a smile.

"Well, not exactly 'good.' See, demons view us as lesser beings. They need us because we can summon them, and to many demons our world is more pleasant and more interesting than theirs. But they can't be permanently killed, and live forever, while we most certainly die. They see themselves as superior and us as more a means to an end. Saeralyx loves art and beauty, but it'll also go on a killing spree to prolong its summoning if it means it can stay here and finish reading a book of poetry."

"Oh, I see," Penny said. "Seems like a horrible way to see the world."

"It's up to interpretation," Roldin said with a shrug. "They sort of think of us as food. How do you think that fish you just ate felt about keeping you alive longer and keeping you from starving to death?"

Penny had no answer to that. Instead she ate more bread, and purposefully left her fish alone. "What did she mean by that title she gave you?" Penny finally asked to cut the silence. "About the seven or five souls, or whatever you two were talking about."

Roldin finished chewing his food and took a long drink of the waterskin. "When I was ten, my father sold my soul to seven demons at the request of Lord Twill, all for a chest of coins. That meant that my soul was claimed by all seven of them, who each had a right to part of it. I've been running from them ever since."

Penny blinked. "How could a father do that to his son?"

"Because he was a bastard," Roldin shrugged. "At least my soul didn't come cheap—those seven demons were summoned to take over the castle at Parvia and won the now royal 'King' Twill a new kingdom. Luckily for me, only one demon survived that first night and took its share. Because of that, I lived another day, then another after that. Another demon caught up to me fifteen years ago. I lost the fight, it took its share. Now there are five left who still think they have a claim to part of me."

"And that's why you're wanted in Adren?"

Roldin nodded. "My guess is the king's in pretty thick with a few of the demons. I wager they pressure him about not being able to collect on me, even now. He'll do whatever he can to appease them. Also, I figured out what happened a while ago and I think he knows that. Can't be good politics to have rumors that he consorts with demons, and especially bad for him to have somebody running around who is living proof of that."

The barmaid sat back and shook her head in disbelief. "And you've run from them all this time?"

"Not all running." He patted the axe at his belt. "I learned to fight back, even how to hunt them and the cultists who worship them. I'm really only in danger when someone happens to summon one of my five over. Sometimes, those five'll do whatever it is they're bid to do as payment from some fool. Then they'll try their best – before their summoning runs out and they're banished back to their world – to find me. Other times, if cultists know I'm near, the five will be summoned just to get me. I'm rather…known… amongst cultist circles. I've learned its best not to make it easy for the demons or their pawns, so I keep moving. Sometimes they'll leave me alone for a bit, other than the dreams they send my way."

"They…send you dreams?"

"The two that have parts of my soul can contact me from the demon realm through dreams, as we share a link. The other demons who claim my soul can go to them and use the connection to torment me, which they've done since I was a boy. The cruelest of them, Yunirax, spoke to me the other day after the night at the tavern. It was…chattier than normal, which made me nervous. Something's going on that I don't understand."

He laughed after a moment. "I will admit that it's slightly insane to be more afraid of conversation than torture."

"That's no way for a child to grow up," Penny said sadly.

"Well, it happened. Nothing can be done for it now," the demon slayer said.

Alys returned wearing an odd ensemble of a plain white dress and what looked like typical university robes, as well as a knit hat that barely fit over her mangled hair and she had painted a happy face on her forehead. "You can't ask," she protested. "It has to do with a bet."

Roldin shrugged and helped her clear a space for her to sit. He walked to the center of the circle they made, took the heartstone out of his pocket, and placed it on the ground. Alys immediately jumped over to it and picked it up, turning it over in her hands and cooing at it. Roldin sighed then unsheathed the one intact dagger he had left and checked the edge for sharpness.

Penny watched her young friend with concern as she studied the heartstone gleefully, especially once Roldin took out the dagger. "Why does Alys have to do this?" she asked him. "Why can't you summon your own damned demons?"

He kept checking the edge of the dagger, not meeting Penny's eyes. "You need blood to do a summoning. It means that even the act of being summoned gives the demons something in return, something they can use to make themselves more powerful. My soul has been…diminished. My blood isn't powerful enough to summon one."

"Whose heartstone is this?" Alys asked inquisitively as she turned the dark rock around in her hands.

"It belonged to Zhannavirik. I fought it three days ago."

She looked up at him sharply. "You're kidding. And you killed it?"

"That's what I do."

Alys jumped up and down in excitement. "Zhannavirik is one of the most powerful demons ever! It was the one summoned a hundred and twenty five—no, a hundred and twenty two—years ago by the Baron of Granchester. It assaulted Penegrin Castle and kidnapped the Duke's son, starting the War of the Bloody Quill." She brought the stone right up to her spectacles, studying it intently. Alys looked up at Roldin quickly, her eyes wide. "Is Zhannavirik one of the ones who…"

He nodded. "Luckily he's not one of the smarter ones."

"Wow," she said. "Out of the three hundred and ninety four known demons, how many do you think you've killed?"

Roldin laughed, and was finally content with the edge of his dagger. "I don't know, I've honestly never kept a tally. But I do have history with a lot of them." He reversed the dagger and handed it to Alys, who took it with an odd look on her face. "Do you know what to do with that?" he asked.

"I think I'm supposed to drip…twenty drops onto the stone?"

"There's no set number, that's an old folk tale," he explained. "Just make a little cut here, on the back of your hand. It'll bleed but not too much. It should be enough."

She took a deep breath. "And who am I calling and what am I promising?"

"You're calling Saeralyx. You are promising it a talk with an old friend."

Alys nodded. With a wince she pulled the dagger over the back of her hand then turned her wrist over immediately. Her blood fell onto the stone, one drop at a time. "Saeralyx, I call you, I call you to talk to an old friend. Saeralyx, I call you, I call you to talk to an old friend. Saeralyx, I call you, I call you to talk to an old friend."

The girl repeated it many times, each time growing a little bit fainter. Penny stepped close to Roldin and whispered, "What's happening to her?"

"The demon is answering," he whispered in return. "She's getting weaker because it's beginning to tug at her life force in order to enter the world. Don't worry, she's doing it correctly, she won't be permanently harmed by it."

Alys continued for a time, growing fainter and fainter. The heartstone on the ground seemed to grow darker, as if a shadow passed over it, but only it. To Penny it felt like it just got harder to see, but nothing around it changed. Finally it vanished entirely, replaced by what looked like a dark shadow on the ground. It began to grow. It seemed to take a shape, and somehow it became a shadow of light instead of darkness.

And then, in the blink of an eye, Saeralyx stood before them.

The demon looked odd—the eyes were too far apart to be human, it had no hair, and while it had two arms and two legs, they ended in three delicate feather-like fingers. Its skin was almost pure white, very smooth, and tinted with flecks of silver. Penny noted that, unlike the horror from the other night, this demon looked like something out of a children's story. Only the red eyes betrayed its demonic nature.

It looked at Alys with an intensely curious expression, and may have even laughed, but it was hard to tell; Alys herself looked weary but also elated at her success. The demon looked over the girl and saw Roldin and Penny standing behind her. Immediately the demon's appearance changed to be more human-like. Its eyes closed in, five fingers formed, and it was wearing a leaf-green tunic that seamlessly emerged from its skin. "Roldin!" it exclaimed in a tone that sounded like three voices — man, woman, and something *else* — singing all at the same time. It rushed over to Roldin and Penny backed away and braced herself for a fight, but the demon embraced the demon slayer intensely.

"It's been too long," Roldin said with a smile as he wrapped his arms around the demon. It dwarfed the man with its tall, though gangly and delicate frame.

"It has, yes," the demon replied. It backed away and looked him over, taking in his injured leg and new scars. His scars it touched tenderly. It shook its head. "I forget how old you humans get so fast. It feels like just the other day you were a boy asking me how to kiss his first girl."

Roldin laughed. "Did you ever finish reading the Pillars of Huvirettica?"

"Oh I did, I did," the demon said delightedly. "It did me good to read that poem." The demon turned and looked at the women in the room. "Look how rude I'm being," it said with an embarrassed shake of its head. It bowed deeply to both of them. Penny curtsied back awkwardly with an odd grin on her face and Alys clapped excitedly. It turned to the small scholar. "And who are you who summoned me so well?"

The girl beamed. "My name is Alys, and I'm from Eganstown! I've studied demons my whole life though I am a little scared of you all but I just find you so fascinating! Can I touch you!?"

Saeralyx's face contorted into a gentle smile as it held its hand out. Alys touched it gingerly at first with a finger, and then put her whole hand on it with wonder on her face. "Wow, you're so cold, and so soft! Is this the form you normally take?"

"When I am around friends, yes, this is what I prefer. It puts people at ease."

"What about when you get angry or need blood? Can I see that?"

Saeralyx shook its head. "I'd rather not, if you don't mind. But I am honored, Alys of Eganstown, to have met you," Saeralyx said with another bow. It looked next at Penny with curiosity.

"Oh, I'm just a barmaid," she said, waving her hand dismissively. "I like cold drinks and a warm fire and never really give demons much thought." Penny pulled her braid around and began fiddling with it absently.

Saeralyx bowed again anyway. It studied its old friend again, its face turning serious. "You need something."

"I do," Roldin admitted. "Three days ago, I fought Zhannavirik and everything seemed as cordial as usual. Then Yunirax came to me in a dream and…well, it wanted something, but I'm not sure what."

"Yunirax, was it?" Saeralyx asked, a bitter look on its face.

"Then the day after, in the town where I was recuperating, five cultists arrived, and they tried to summon five demons in the middle of the town, meant for me, but Yunirax was the only name I recognized. The cultists said something about 'plans have changed' and seemed to hint at something else. Do you know what any of that means?"

Saeralyx sighed — it sounded like birds crying. "I've heard whispers the last two days. They've been after you a long time, Roldin. Even for demons. Your soul was such an amazingly valuable treasure when you were a boy, even split seven ways. But now, after so long, it's not worth so much to them. They've gone from wanting your soul as their prize to wanting your soul out of spite, as a token of personal pride. I don't know why, exactly. There's something going around that even I have not been able to discern, but the mood there is volatile.

"Normally, it would be considered impossibly uncouth for a demon to take a soul marked for another. Your soul can be doled out after the demon returns to our realm, but it won't be as powerful. The five have decided that decorum will not matter. They want your soul. If they can, they will appear together to retrieve it. If not, they are content to accept it from another demon, and they will even allow the demon who took it from you to keep part of it as a reward."

Roldin shrugged in disbelief. "So there's a demon's bounty on my soul?" Alys, still seated, scooted away from him slowly with wide eyes.

"In a manner of speaking, yes," Saeralyx replied. "You have made many enemies here with your actions over the years. A few have spent a long time wishing they could have killed you instead of holding back for fear of reprisal from their fellows. I'm afraid you are in more danger now than ever."

The demon slayer sighed. "I guess there's not much I can do to reason with them, is there? Zhannavirik must have spread the word of where he caught up to me quickly. The other day it was five cultists…tomorrow it could be worse."

"I'm sorry, I truly am," Saeralyx said, tracing its hands affectionately down Roldin's face. "You've come so far, lasted so long…perhaps, perhaps I can go talk to some of them. Your five, especially Yunirax and Corbannus, are not much loved here for their exceeding brutality. I could perhaps convince some that they will rescind on their bargain if your bounty was to be collected."

Roldin took Saeralyx's hands and gripped them. "Anything to buy me some time would be a gift," he said. "Enough for me to get on the move, away from Road's End."

The demon nodded and touched Roldin on the forehead with a finger. Then it stepped back, seemed to reach inside its own body, and presented its heartstone in its hand before the demon slayer. "Send me back now and I will do what I can, my old friend."

"Thank you again," Roldin said as he pulled out his weapon and poised it gently above the upraised stone. "Maybe I'll see you soon." He raised his axe and, with a carefully calculated strike, cracked the heartstone. It dropped to the ground and shattered, and Saeralyx's physical form evaporated into white smoke that fell heavy and billowed upon the ground before vanishing altogether.

Roldin put his axe back on his belt and turned to face the women behind him. Neither said anything. His throat was dry. "Is there an easy way over these mountains?" he asked them. "That would be the quickest way to put something between me and the town." He shuffled over to a fallen stone pillar and sat down heavily, rubbing his leg absently.

"Not that I know of," Alys said, and Penny shook her

head as well.

"Maybe I could find a horse, ride straight south," he mused, shaking his head in thought. "Ride anywhere…"

"It's not fair," Penny said. "Haven't they put you through enough?" The demon slayer didn't respond.

Penny helped Alys bandage her hand and stand up. The scholar was a little woozy but none too worse for wear. "Alys, do you know anything in your studies that could help him? Something you've read?"

The woman thought for a moment, then shook her head. She was pale, and not just from blood loss. "This…I don't think this kind of thing has ever happened before. Souls are always collected strictly by the one who has a mark. To not obey that is unheard of. If any demon at all could collect on a soul…"

"But there's not any kind of loophole? Anything?"

Alys frowned and her eyes shimmered slightly behind her spectacles. "Demon marking by itself is a rather common thing throughout history. It's rare for a child, since it would take…" she glanced at Roldin and her voice got quieter, "since it would take a truly despicable person to give up their own child, but none of those stories has a happy ending, and most are over in a matter of days, if not hours. For him to survive for over thirty years is…it's unheard of."

Penny sighed and crossed her arms. "There must be something. Roldin can you—" She looked over at the demon slayer and saw that he was slumped forward, not moving. Both women rushed over to him quickly. "He's burning up," Penny said.

As Alys bent down to examine him she put one hand on his leg, but she withdrew it quickly. "His leg is on fire," she said.

"We have to get him back to the medicine woman," Penny said. "Help me get him to the skiff."

"We can use my cart," Alys said.

They both bent down to get the demon slayer to his feet. "No," Roldin groaned, already shaking with fever. "Keep me away…"

"Not today, you stubborn mule," Penny growled. Together the two women carried him to Alys' empty handcart. As soon as he was on his back he lost consciousness.

CHAPTER 6

A PAUSE

Roldin woke, once again, to his own coughs. He forced himself to open his eyes, noticed he was in Old Nanny's hut once more, and groaned quietly.

It was dark outside. Only the fireplace lit the small room. The demon slayer saw a cup next to him that he picked up and sniffed. He recognized a handful of herbs and roots meant to quell fever. He did feel better, he had to admit. Even his leg was less swollen, though still in pain.

There was a sound to his right. He turned his head quickly and saw Penny, asleep and stirring softly, in the chair next to him. Roldin shook his head. *She should not have brought me back here*, he thought. His gear and axe were nearby. *If I could retrieve them quietly enough and slip away….*

He knew he wasn't that crafty at the moment. He'd be more likely to trip and fall now than to sneak anywhere, but his presence was a danger and that was not something he wanted to have on his conscience. Roldin lay back in exhaustion, closed his eyes, and tried to think of a plan.

Something stirred in his gut. The hair on his neck went on end, and his knee jerked. He knew that something was above him. Penny groaned in her sleep. Roldin tried to calculate how far he would have to leap to reach his axe, how he would do it with his leg, and how he could protect Penny, all without getting torn to shreds. *There is no use in delaying any longer*, he thought to himself. He opened his eyes.

There was nothing but darkness. The fireplace was either blocked by something large or winked out, or…

No, something was clouding his vision utterly.

He could hear air rush past his ears. There was a cloud of mist covering him, and it was racing around his head like a maelstrom. He lifted his hands and could feel it stream through his fingers, impossibly cold. Again he wondered how he could reach his axe. This demon would have to turn from mist into something more solid if it wanted to hurt him, and he would not have much time to react when it did.

The mist spinning in front of his face began to reveal light. He wasn't sure where the glow came from, except from the demon itself. It twirled and swirled, and he began to make out patterns from within. A picture seemed to form: a red sky with churning, angry clouds and a ground filled with dark stones. It looked like a rocky valley made of heartstones.

And then a form took shape, walking in the field of black and red. It looked very much like the shape of a woman, with skin as pale as death and a dress of wispy red silk that swirled around her. Its face changed from one woman to another, blinking at random, seemingly adjusting itself. Women he'd known? He wasn't sure. It finally settled on a surpassingly beautiful face, and despite everything going on around him, he found his heart ached at her loveliness.

She opened her eyes. They were crimson and cold.

"Hello, Roldin," the demon said in a voice that was of

the mist that surrounded him, filling his ears in a way that was uncomfortably intrusive. He knew the voice, recognized it from the dreams it sends. Not that he would need to hear it to know what demon this was—only one demon was so skilled in form manipulation to put on a show like this.

"Yunirax," he said quietly.

"And so I have reached you first," it said in a voice of purring impurity. He would attribute "she" to the voice that was inside his head, not to mention the vision it formed in front of his eyes. "Do you remember the last time we met?"

"It wasn't so long ago," he said, trying to prevent his voice from shaking. "Three years? You had disguised yourself as a woman inside the court at Kullen's Bay. I was called in by one of the dukes who I owed a favor to try to figure out what kind of demonic force was haunting his castle. I exposed you for what you were, I killed you, and I think I danced on the crumbled ruin of your heartstone at the end."

"But not before I had killed eight guards and three chambermaids, and had seduced the duke's sister," the form purred at him. "Such failure, demon slayer, to protect those around you."

Roldin sneered. "You make a very convincing –"

"Careful now, boy, you forget who you speak to," Yunirax said. The red sky in front of Roldin's eyes churned dangerously. "Though I am as you say, and yet, I am so much more," it said. The woman in the vision before his eyes smiled. "We have much more history than that, you know."

"Of course we do," he said. "Have you come to collect your fifth? Or take all of them back to your cohorts? Do what you will, demon, and get it over with."

"Oh, such manners, Roldin," Yunirax said, as the form in front of his eyes shook its head. "If I wanted you dead I wouldn't be here like this. I've come to you first, before the rest, to offer you something."

Roldin laughed mirthlessly. "You have nothing I want."

"I want to offer you peace."

Roldin fell silent. "...I'm listening."

"I know you are," Yunirax purred, and the lady vision before him reached out a hand. One of the tendrils of mist reached out from its swirling dance and touched his face; making his jaw go numb. "I respect you, Roldin. You may not think so, but I do. You evaded us for so long, even as a small child. Then you fought back with the tenacity of a demon yourself. You have done your race proud for so very long. But you're older now. Your soul has been corrupted by the evils of your people, by their weaknesses and their fears."

The lady before him closed her eyes contentedly and smiled at him. "Aren't you tired? Don't you long to rest, dear boy? Don't you want to sleep a full night without a part of you lying awake, scared, waiting for one of us to catch up to you? Maybe find a home somewhere, and leave the road behind you? Don't you want to put down your weapons and live a life of peace?" Roldin did not want to admit the feelings that the demon stirred up. A tear formed in one eye and was instantly swept away by the churning mist surrounding him. "I can offer you that. A truce, a peace, from me and from the other four. I promise this to you."

"And what do you want for this peace?"

"What do you think?" it asked. The woman opened her eyes and the demon slayer was transfixed by her red, hungry stare. "A soul. A young soul. Your *son's* soul."

Roldin shook his head. "I don't have a son."

"Do you not?" it asked. The mist parted and revealed the sleeping form of Penny in the chair next to him. "I told you to open your eyes, boy."

"Linder," he whispered and shook his head violently. "No, no it's not true…"

"Ask her," Yunirax said. "She will not deny it."

"No, I won't," Roldin said with a growl.

"And why not?" the demon asked, once again obscuring Penny and forming the scarlet-eyed woman's face in front of him. "What is the boy to you? How many short hours have you spent in his presence? You won't even miss him. You are his father…you can give him to us. I will take his soul now, tonight; he will not suffer for years as you have. It will be quick, merciful. One drop of his blood, one drop of yours, a promise of his soul, and it will be done. She will think he died in his sleep. She is young enough to bear herself another. And you will be free, Roldin. Finally free of the road…"

"I wo—" and to his horror and shame, Roldin heard himself pause.

The demon before him smiled. "You know yourself, slayer. What could this boy be to you? You walk your paths alone. You aren't capable of loving someone other than yourself. He could never love one as steeped in death and violence as you are. Your darkness has tainted you, and what's left of your soul has grown black with your despair."

Roldin shut his eyes and shook his head against her cold red gaze.

"Think on it," Yunirax said. "But you will not have long. We are coming, you know. To this town. Road's End. You could run to the other end of the world tonight and we would still stop here to kill everyone in this town and trample its ashes on our way to you, just to cause you guilt. You've already doomed this place with your selfishness. Think on it, Roldin Benirus. One life—one small, young soul—for yours, and the lives of this whole town." Something in the red eyes before him bored into what remained of his soul. It began to whisper to him. "The others think me foolish. They say you will run, like you always have. I hope you're smarter than that. You have one day until the rest arrive."

The mist-formed woman before him closed her demon eyes and seemed to lean in to kiss him. Mist swirled closer, touching his lips briefly, numbing them. Then the mist lifted, flew through a crack in a window, and was gone.

The demon slayer lay still in the bed until his breathing returned to normal. He was suddenly very thirsty. Roldin reached for a water cup near the bed and knocked it over onto the floor. Penny stirred and woke.

"Roldin, are you all right?" she asked. She bent down and retrieved the cup, poured water in it, and put it to his lips gently so he could drink deep. It felt odd and uninviting on his still numb lips. Penny felt his forehead with her hand. "Your fever is gone."

It was such a motherly action that it nearly undid him. He reached up and removed her hand. It lingered on hers, a little longer than he intended, and she took it back gently and looked away.

"Penny," he said, his voice hoarse. "Is he mine?"

She turned back to him in shock. Her eyebrows narrowed and Roldin could see the beginning of a sharp retort on her lips. Then, she suddenly deflated. "Yes," she said quietly. Penny sunk back down in the chair opposite his bed. "I didn't want to tell you, because, I guess it didn't matter."

They were both silent. Penny was playing with the hem of her dress. Roldin could clearly hear the sound of the rain against the window and his heart beating in his chest. She finally said, "After you left Levin's Ferry I didn't tell anyone the details. I was too ashamed. Hells, I even tried to deny it to myself enough times that I sort of willed myself to forget."

Roldin couldn't help but bristle. "I couldn't have been that bad."

Penny laughed. "No, it wasn't that. I had just let myself be weak and…anyway, not long afterwards it was apparent to me what had happened. Then I started to show. I began to tell people that I had slept with you and, for some reason, no one believed me. 'No, not the brave and honorable demon slayer, Krill Tempest!' they'd say. They thought because I hadn't said anything earlier that I was making it up. Half the town thought I was sleeping around with every man in sight, and the other half thought that a demon had come for me after all and impregnated me."

"That's absurd," Roldin said.

"They don't understand demons, they're simple country town folk," Penny said. "Not many people do, in general. But that explanation made sense to them. My parents didn't know what to think and stopped listening to me. Finally I realized it was no use. I left— just me and my belly. Kept walking until I got here, the actual end of the road. Found a job at the tavern. Old Nanny here helped me give birth in this very house, and I've been here ever since."

Roldin shook his head. "You know I…I live my life feeling sorry for myself, thinking that I suffered so much that the world owed me happiness. I went around, taking what I could of life's pleasures, not really thinking of any of the consequences. I'm s—"

"Don't," she said sharply. "Don't you dare give me your pity. You wronged me, yes, but Linder…Linder is the best thing that ever happened to me. Before him I was a scared girl who didn't know what I wanted to do with myself or my life, long before you swaggered into town. After Linder, though, my whole life just made sense. So don't you dare be sorry for that."

Penny rubbed her face with her hands, then laughed. "He keeps asking about you. I think he likes you," she shook her head. "Why did you think to ask?"

"I just…I guess I saw a lot of me in him the other day: the books, the attitude, the eyes. I just wondered." He smiled at her, but the unspoken horror of what he was considering bore down on his soul so heavily that he thought he would be shamed into oblivion.

#

Penny left him to sleep. Dawn came and he was still unsure of what he would do. A few of the townspeople greeted him as he slowly made his way down the plankways of Road's End, leaning on his crutch, watching the town in silence. None questioned where he had been the past two days. None suspected the storm that was coming. None knew how much of a danger walked among them.

One life for many was the deal. He observed the citizens of Road's End go about their daily lives. Off-season miners-turned-fishermen scrambled into boats, their large rock-crushing muscles straining around tiny fishing poles, just to make a living. A handful of children ran around, ignoring the early morning drizzle, and played with wooden swords or threw things at each other amidst laughter and boyish taunting. A happy couple sat just inside the front door of their house, the woman nestled in her man's lap while she cradled his head in affection, feeding each other breakfast.

None suspected the death that would visit them on the morrow.

His mood grew darker, and a few of the townspeople who walked by could sense it. They shrunk away from the glare of the odd visitor who did not belong. Roldin paused at the end of the plankways and looked down the main thoroughfare at the flooded waters beyond the town. He turned his eyes downward and watched the water swirl beneath the wooden planks under his feet, oblivious to anything but its own nature. The demon slayer could already imagine the river red with innocent blood.

"Hi Gaeryn," he heard from behind him. Roldin didn't have to turn to know that it was Linder. He felt his heart stop. "What are you doing?"

The demon slayer didn't dare look at him. He knew his emotions would be too plain on his face. "Just thinking, Linder," he responded.

"This is my favorite place to think, too," the boy said. He stood next to Roldin and watched the water go by, too, mimicking his father's posture without meaning to.

"You should go," Roldin said quietly.

"I don't have anywhere to be—"

"Go away, Linder!" the demon slayer yelled, louder and fiercer than he meant to, and the boy jumped back. The look on Linder's face gripped his heart. It was a look he'd never seen before, but he'd felt the same expression on his own face a thousand times as a child after being yelled at much like that. The boy turned and ran.

Roldin's sneer grew on his face like a feral snarl. The man looked back down to the flood waters going by and wondered, not for the first time, if it would be deep enough to drown him. Could something as simple as water be the end of Roldin Benirus? *How many problems in the world that would solve*, he thought darkly.

More importantly, he thought, the demons would lose out on his soul. It was the simplest solution. The thought made the blood rush in his veins. Exhilaration blinded him and the thrill of victory was a tangible taste on his tongue. Then the same nagging truth he realized every time he went down this road crept back into his heart. It was a simple thing that held him back like strong hands as he knelt over the edge of a waterfall: he didn't want to die. The demons would lose, but Roldin wouldn't win. He was trapped in his own scarred, tired body, and there was nothing he could do about it until he simply failed at his life-long quest to defend himself. The demon slayer held back a growl in his throat.

There was an instant, as he watched the waters beneath, when he could see his reflection against the light grey sky behind him, and the man he saw was not himself — the frowning, disdainful face of his father stared back at him.

Roldin looked away, suddenly dizzy. All the fears of his life were coming to pass and he felt powerless to stop any of it. Yunirax's words echoed in his ears like a broken bell. He gripped the railing of the plankway tightly to steady himself and could still see Linder running from his words, racing further across the town. His breaths came in ragged, shallow gulps.

He looked back into the water and saw his own reflection — not the face of a man, but of a little boy, running and scared for reasons he didn't understand.

Roldin had not thought of the child he used to be for a long time. That young boy would not give up another person to save himself. *But it's not just myself now, is it?* he realized. Roldin rubbed his hands together, trying to get some feeling in his numb fingers. He looked down at his leg and cursed it. *If only I had left sooner. If only I had never met Penny and Linder.* Every life here was over, and the only way to save them was on Roldin's shoulders — if he gave over the soul of his son.

That thought finally, all of a sudden, hit him full in the gut. *I have a son!* he thought with an unbidden laugh. A little boy, smart and precocious, was his. Since his own childhood he'd wondered what kind of father he would make. He had promised himself he would be kind where his father had been stern and that he would be generous where his father had been stingy, among a thousand other wrongs he would make right. Roldin had promised all the Sacreds and himself that he would love his children in ways that he never had been.

And now, unexpectedly, he had that chance — a chance to do things right.

His smile faded as elation left him and reality sunk in again. He had made those promises but, then again, that was never a real possibility, was it? How could he raise a child when his soul was forfeit and he was constantly moving and always fighting? It had been a dream that warmed him on cold nights when he was alone and wished he had a father who loved him.

What would it matter if he let yet another one of his dreams die? It would save a town from destruction, and he would get to stop running. It was the only choice.

I get to stop running, he thought, *but I lose my soul anyway.*

His mind was made up that quickly. "No," he

growled to himself. "Not the only choice."

"Roldin Benirus!" a voice called out from behind him.

Roldin turned quickly before he remembered that his name was supposed to be Gaeryn Blackthorn. He came face-to-face with Constable Jodas, his spear hefted in sweating hands, and a few of the more burly miners around him with some antique-looking swords. Wull was behind them, wringing his hands like he always did, and said, "I read that it was on the back of his neck."

Jodas straightened. "Pardon me, demon slayer, but you have been accused of being a man by the name of Roldin Benirus, fugitive to Adren. I need you to turn around." The four men with swords walked forward slowly. A few of the townspeople began to gather around to watch.

Roldin knew better than to resist. He turned around and lifted his dark mop of hair. On the back of his neck, faded but still visible, was the beginning of a branding scar meant to mark criminals in the kingdom of Adren. Jodas approached cautiously and examined it. "Only part of it is there—it's meant to be branded around the entire neck."

"That's as much as I let them do," the demon slayer replied with a shrug. "They didn't get to hold me for long."

Jodas cleared his throat and backed away from the demon slayer's reach. "Under the authority of his majesty King Twill of Adren I place you, Roldin Benirus, under arrest for the charges of forgery, perjury, conspiracy against the government, and murder." One of the other miners removed Roldin's axe, and all four of them grabbed his arms tightly.

"Throw me in jail if you want," the demon slayer said, "but I need to talk to the mayor. Now."

Jodas shook his head. "Your defense is best served to his majesty's lawmen, who will be coming to fetch you as soon as we send word."

"What I have to say does not concern my defense," he said, pleading with Jodas, eye to eye, "but the defense of the entire town."

Thirty Two Years Earlier

He'd allowed himself a nap during the day while the sun was warm, and his exhaustion was so oppressive and his sleep so blessedly free of nightmares that he lingered in a deep slumber for the entirety of the day. He was woken by the crunch of something moving through the dried leaves around the log he'd hid himself under, and he opened his eyes to see nothing but the inky blackness of night surrounding him.

He immediately realized what he'd done and he would have kicked himself for his carelessness if he'd had the courage to move. The ringing in his ears was accompanied by a sheen of sweat that chilled his small frame as the wind came barreling through his tiny hiding spot. Something large was moving, slowly, near to him. Heavy steps crushed leaf and twig alike. In the stillness of the night the sounds made Roldin's skin crawl, and every crunch made his wide eyes wince.

He could hear breathing now as the thing moved closer to where he lay, and he knew immediately that whatever it was, it wasn't human. A guttural growl accompanied each exhale, along with a wheezing sound that reeked of desperation. It came closer to his log; so close that the hollow wood shook from the steps.

Luck — or maybe the Sacreds — saved him. From off in the distance Roldin heard laughing — a man's voice, and a woman's both. The creature near him stopped and was still for a moment, before it began a slow stomp off towards the sounds. Not long

120

after it moved away, Roldin had no choice. Even though his stomach was cramped with hunger and his breathing was as weak and as rasping as the creature's, he jumped up and ran in the opposite direction.

Maybe he'd not waited long enough, or it knew where he was, but immediately he felt something pursuing him again and leaving the laughing couple behind. Roldin chanced a glance behind him and saw a dark, hungry, and growling form barreling down on him. Though the forest was dark and the moonlight and starlight was mostly hidden by the canopy of leaves above, he could clearly see dark blue scales, shimmering as if they were wet, and a set of dark claws on mangled hands. The boy looked straight ahead and let fear lead him over downed limbs and rocks on the forest floor without losing his footing. The creature pursuing him simply smashed through trees, splintering them into kindling.

One of the wooden splinters nicked the back of Roldin's neck, and he could feel blood ooze down his back and under his tunic. He didn't even spare the breath to scream from the pain, keeping his panicked gaze ahead. The boy felt a sudden rush of air and knew the creature was right behind him and had swiped at him, barely missing the back of his head. Somehow, with power borne of sheer desperation, he ran faster.

Abruptly the sound of footsteps and breathing stopped. The forest ached in the unexpected quiet. Roldin risked another glance backwards and saw nothing behind him but a trail of broken trees. He let himself fall to the ground, his breaths coming in loud gasps. He didn't bother to wipe the unbidden tears that came to him – the strain of his hasty flight was too much. The boy lay back on the ground and tried to catch his breath. He looked up at the starry sky above him.

It was gone.

He cocked his head to one side, unsure of what he was seeing. It was as if black clouds covered not only the moon, but the trees and limbs above him as well. Instinct told him to move, and that he did, rolling to the side just as the black cloud slammed into the ground where he had been laying. The boy watched in horror as it shifted along the forest floor and billowed up into a shape that no cloud could hope to achieve, and a scaled arm formed out of the mist and grabbed at him. Glowing red eyes peered at him from the darkness.

It grabbed his leg. The claws were cold and sharp, and bit into his skin. His eyes wide with terror, Roldin reached around for something – anything – and his hand found a loose rock. With a movement that was anything but graceful, he struck with his newfound weapon and hit the scaled arm. It shook under the blow. Roldin thought he heard laughter coming from the cloud which, with every passing moment, seemed to shift into something more solid.

He repeated the strike and, finally, hit it with enough force that the hand shrank back and the creature growled in pain. Roldin scrambled to his feet and ran, but the creature was faster as a cloud than it was as a lumbering beast. It vaulted up into the air and landed in front of him. The boy leapt to the side, and his foot found a rock that tripped him. A tendril of cloud lashed at where his head had been. He had been lucky, but he knew that would only last so long.

Roldin dodged another pillar of dark cloud, and another, just trying to move forward, away. In the darkness of night he didn't see the river in front of him until he was already in it, falling head first into the chilly waters. Its current swept him away, and as he was tossed and turned by the swift waters he could see the creature pursuing, growing darker and more cloudlike as it rushed through the air after him. Wind ripped at the darkness, threatening to disperse it into the night, but somehow it held itself together in ways he couldn't understand.

The river was too fast and he outpaced the creature. The boy had learned to swim but fought just to keep his head above water. The current dragged him inexorably downriver. He looked back and could see the dark cloud coming for him, following the river, but before his very eyes it seemed to fade from view. It grew fainter and fainter, and he thought he could hear a deep growl of frustration, and then it was gone. The ringing in his ears and the frantic beating of his heart instantly stopped, and he knew the Dread had left him. Though he couldn't tell, he thought he could see something fall from midair and plop into the water with a splash. But then the river rushed over his head and he had to struggle for breath once more, and he was simply fighting for survival.

The river calmed as it rounded a bend, and he saw a bridge up ahead. He swam as fast as he could towards the shore and emerged from the water, bleeding, shivering, and crying. Roldin saw road signs pointing back towards Neppeth. Though he'd tried to avoid roads in the last two weeks, he crawled up the riverbank and found a tree to rest against. Just a moment, he promised himself. Just a moment of rest before he would think of his next move. Just a moment...

Roldin awoke to the sound of wagon wheels and a familiar rocking movement. For one brief, fleeting second he thought he was back in his father's cart, and that this whole thing had been a bad dream. Of course it had been – none of it had made sense. His father wouldn't have left him like that. Roldin allowed himself a smile and he opened his eyes.

He was in a cart, but it was filled with huy, not barrels and chests. The boy sat up with a start and surprised a woman sitting next to him.

"Quiet dear, it's all right," she told him. She was plain looking, but she had kind eyes. A man was driving the cart, and there was a little girl sitting next to him who was making a cat's cradle out of a piece of string and humming softly.

"Where..." be began. He looked around and saw farmland. The sun was barely in the sky, so it was still before midmorning. He hadn't been out for long.

"We found you on the side of the road, face down in the mud. Worried you were dead but then you moved," the lady said, handing him an apple. He took it numbly. He was covered in blankets and his ever-growing tangle of hair was drying from his swim the night before. "Why are you running away, boy? Where are your parents?" she asked. Roldin could see the man and the girl both turn and look at him curiously.

"I...my father..." he began, and his eyes welled up again with unbidden tears. It wasn't that he didn't want to tell them what happened; it was that he still didn't understand it himself. "My father is...dead. I'm alone."

"Oh, dear," she said, and reached out a hand to pat down his dirty brown hair. Roldin recoiled instinctively. The two adults shared a look, and the little girl smiled at him. The man nodded and the woman turned back to him with a warm smile. "Why don't you come stay with us? We have a spare bedroom. Our oldest son just left to join the legion. You look a tough lad, if a bit scrawny — we could use you at the farm. You wouldn't owe us nothin' but a few hours' work a day."

Roldin looked from the woman, to the man, to the girl. They looked happy, like they could be trusted. He'd never lived in a house and he'd always wanted to. These two didn't sneer at him like his father had. They looked kind, and the idea of being in one place instead of always on the road, to be somewhere long enough to make friends...

He opened his mouth to accept. He wanted to, with every fiber of his being. But as the boy was going to say the word he imagined the smiling man with his throat torn away, imagined the woman and the girl running through their house, chased by some horror, left to a fate better unseen. He imagined their son, coming home from the legion, finding his family murdered.

"No, I can't," he muttered. He said it so quietly that he had to repeat himself.

"Now, now, don't be scared," the woman said soothingly. "We're a friendly sort. Always wanted another son..."

"No!" he screamed. He couldn't take their pitying glances, and he was afraid if she touched his hair like that again that he wouldn't be able to say no anymore. "Leave me alone!" he yelled, and leapt out the back of the cart. The woman called to the man to stop but Roldin had already dashed into the forest and into the brush beside the road. It wasn't the first time he'd leapt from a moving cart, and he knew it wouldn't be his last.

He didn't allow himself time to think as he ran from the woman's soothing pleas, so he ended up following his own footsteps back to Neppeth as the sun set. The city walls had a pall to them that sent shivers down his spine, but he didn't know where else to go. He didn't know if anywhere else was safe anyway.

As he sat there in the growing dark, with the sounds of the forest heavy around him, he began to regret not saying yes. His young mind, confused and hungry and lonely, tormented him as much as any demons ever could.

CHAPTER 7

TRAPPED

"You did *what*?"

"He's a fugitive, Penny," Wull said, patting down his brow with his apron. "I know what he did for the town, but as soon as he walked in here I thought I recognized him from wanted posters I saw over in Neppeth last year."

"And what, you want a reward? Do you really think Adren is going to send you coin?" Penny never took her glare away from the portly barkeep as she continued scrubbing the top of the bar, hard. Wull glanced down and imagined his face being polished under her rags and he gulped involuntarily.

"I couldn't in good conscience let him go free. I heard of the things he did!"

"You heard lies, most like," she sneered. She threw down the rag and stormed out of the bar. "I'm going to stop this farce now before anyone does anything foolish," Penny called out behind her as she went out the door.

A few townspeople stopped to say good morning to her, but they instead had to quickly step to one side as she stomped by them in a huff. The jail was only a few rows down, an open air building that had a nook for the constable to sit on one side and a reinforced cell on the other. It was not a marvel of modern engineering but it served its common clientele in Road's End, who were usually drunken miners.

Penny noticed with a narrowing of her eyes that the muscle-bound men that stood guard outside Roldin's cell were the same ones who often occupied the other side of those same bars. Jodas saw her coming through the crowd and he lifted his hands in a placating gesture. "Penny, I don't know what you heard..."

"Oh, shut your mouth, Jodas," she said to him, dismissingly.

"Penny!" the demon slayer said as she came near. "Listen, you need to get the mayor for me—"

"No one's getting the mayor," the constable said sternly. "I told you where we stood."

"Open this cell," Penny warned Jodas. "He's injured and needs to be in Nanny's hut, resting. You're being foolish about this. Since when have you cared a thing about what Adren thought, anyway? I've heard you grumbling drunkenly at the bar on more than one occasion."

Jodas tried to put a finger to his mouth to shush her but she wasn't paying attention. "Roldin, we're going to get you out of here, do you hear me?"

"Penny, there's no time..." Roldin said, and grabbed for her hand through the bars.

More townspeople had heard the yelling and were gathering outside the walkway to the jail, craning their necks to see in. A few were shouting questions and accusations. Jodas was beginning to get flustered. "I am the law here," he said. He swallowed hard. "This man is imprisoned because he is a fugitive wanted by Adren!"

The people began talking at once, demanding

answers.

"It's true!" Roldin called out to those assembled. "I am a fugitive to Adren. But it's not me you should be worried about!"

Penny put a hand on Roldin's arm through the bars. "You don't have to do this," she said quietly. "I'll figure out some way to get you out of here."

"It's more complicated than that," he said quietly. "I can't leave now."

"Why? What's happened?" she asked, but Roldin could only shake his head.

The crowd was getting restless. Mayor Kinnley finally appeared among the throngs, and Penny waved him over hurriedly. "I've spoken to Wull," he said to her. "If this man is guilty of what he says..."

"Mayor, listen," Roldin said quickly. "You need to let me out but not for the reasons you might think."

Kinnley put a hand up to silence him. "Are you this Benirus? And are you guilty of what they say?"

Roldin sighed. "I am him. But as for the charges... well, actually, that depends. What are they saying now?"

"I believe the warrant currently says 'forgery, perjury, conspiracy against the government, and murder.'"

"Ah, only the murder, then."

The mayor looked at Roldin askance. "That's not helping."

"They weren't very nice men and to be fair, they tried to kill me first—listen, that's not important right now." Roldin looked over the mayor's shoulder and saw that most of the townspeople had gathered.

"People of Road's End!" he called out. Slowly, the

people quieted and looked his way.

"I lied before, I lied to all of you," he said. Roldin couldn't find a good place to put his arms, so he just left them by his side and took a deep breath. "My name is not Blackthorn. It is Roldin Benirus. I am a demon slayer, like I said, and there was a demon coming to Road's End the other night, like I said. But it was coming for me."

Several of the townspeople started yelling or talking amongst themselves. Roldin saw Clariya's father push his way forward with an angry look on his face. "What do you mean coming for you? You mean you endangered my daughter for nothing?"

"Yes, I did," Roldin admitted. "I...thought she was pretty." He shrugged, but that only made the old man angrier. The demon slayer swallowed and turned back to the crowd. "There are more of them coming, tomorrow, also for me. And they will destroy the whole town to get me."

Penny's eyes widened as she stood next to him. Jodas stepped forward. "How do we know you're not just saying this so we set you free?"

The crowd erupted in panic and drowned out the constable's words. "Why don't you just leave!" one of the townspeople yelled.

"Because my running will do no good," he said. "Even if I leave they will destroy the town. My presence here has damned all of you."

"We should run! Evacuate the town!" someone screamed. Affirmations ran around the assembly.

The mayor heard and shouted, "The flood waters are too high, we'd never get all of us out quickly enough or far enough away in time to make a difference," he said. "If we get caught out in the middle of the woods, defenseless, we'll stand no chance at all." Kinnley shrugged helplessly. "If what you say is true, we're trapped," he said, quietly, and only to Roldin.

The demon slayer shook his head. "We can defend the town," he shouted so his voice could be heard above the alarmed throng. "I will not abandon it. I have killed demons for longer than some of you have been alive. I will stand here and I will fight them." He scanned the townspeople and met every eye in the crowd. "I will not let this town fall."

"But you're just one man," old man Silas yelled. "What could you do?"

"Not just one!" a high-pitched voice called out. Alys edged her way out of the crowd and stood near his cell. "I mean, I'm not a man, so technically it's one man and one woman, but I've seen traps made at the university, and I've studied centuries of demon battles. I can help!"

Roldin looked at her in shock as the town erupted once again in alarm. "You're still here?" he asked her.

"And miss this?" she said with a trill-like laugh. "I stay for all the good parties."

A few of the townspeople recognized her and groaned. "A dead man and a mad woman," some of them grumbled. A couple of them defended her. As the voices grew more panicked Jodas stepped forward and called for silence. None listened, so he pounded the butt of his spear on the plankways in an attempt to restore order.

He called out above the din, "We don't know if he's telling the truth. And if he is, he has already put us all in danger with his lies!" People argued even louder amongst themselves, trying to drown each other out.

"I do not refute that," Roldin said to Jodas. "I know I have brought this upon you. We don't have much time, but we know they're coming. We have time to prepare, and they won't expect that. Let me help you."

Penny saw Kinnley rubbing his eyes helplessly and Jodas unsuccessfully managing the crowd. She shook her head against the madness. "He may be guilty of lying to us but he's innocent of what Adren claims!" Penny yelled, getting the attention of many. "The truth is far simpler. Roldin killed a demon, a very powerful demon, in my taproom not so long ago," she continued. "I was here and I saw. This whole town has been singing his praises and for good reason. He may have not told us his name, but can you blame him? He's wanted by a corrupt law and by demons that have chased him all his life. He's still injured from his fight in there, when that monster could have run rampant and killed us all. Now he wants to do it again, to kill demons trying to kill us, and you're going to turn your back on him?" Penny used her signature steely-eyed gaze on the assembled townsfolk. "If that's so then this is not the same community that took me in all those years ago!"

Some of the town actually looked chastened by the barmaid. Others continued to panic. The constable looked over at Roldin, who gripped the cell bars and tried to think of what else he could say to the crowd. Jodas turned and met the mayor's gaze, then Penny's earnest one. "His innocence is not for me to decide," he said with a shrug. The constable looked down for many moments, and finally shook his head. "But what is for me to decide," Jodas yelled, puffing up his chest and giving his best authoritative sneer, finally silencing the crowd, "is that I think Adren is a kingdom of cheats and liars and tyrants." Several of the townspeople yelled their agreements; others gasped at the display of treason. "I may be an officer of the law, but I say any enemy of Adren is a friend of mine. Penny is right that he is real." He turned to the demon slayer and, reluctantly, bowed his head. "I will fight with you, Roldin Benirus."

A wave of support washed over the demon slayer. The mayor looked around in awe. "Your name may be different," Kinnley said, "but I still saw the kind of repairs that had to be made to the inn the other day. I'll fight with you, as well."

Though the crowd was still divided, most cheered as Jodas reached around and unlocked the cell. The mayor put a hand on the demon slayer's chest as he exited. "This better not be some kind of trick," he warned.

"Mayor, I promise you," he said, as he shook his head and laughed. "This is one of the only honest things I've done my entire life." Roldin gripped Kinnley's hand and nodded. "I will not fail this town."

Penny approached them and sighed. "I'm going to have to take something out of Wull's hide," she said.

Roldin smiled at her. "Thanks for the support."

"Of course," she said with a wry smile. "So, we're being invaded by demons?" she asked conversationally.

"We are," he said. "It's not looking very promising."

Kinnley sighed and looked out at the gathered crowd, who were still talking amongst themselves in varying degrees of panic. "We're not warriors here."

"You won't have to be," Roldin promised.

The mayor nodded. "Then what's your plan?"

The demon slayer looked to Alys, who grinned at him, a little too widely for his liking. Roldin nodded his head, "I think we have a few. Shall we meet in your office?"

"Well, I don't have an office, as we are an incredibly small town, but I do have a study. That will have to suffice." The mayor addressed Jodas. "Calm these people down. Take your thugs over there and have them restore order, peacefully. If anyone asks tell them we'll address them soon."

"Yes sir," the constable said and saluted. He extended his hand to Roldin. "I'm sorry for all this," he said. "Got caught up in my job, I suppose."

"You did what you thought was right," Roldin said with a smile and shook his hand. He leaned in close and lowered his voice. "By the way, there are five dead cultists in the basement of the Crawsons' old house," he quickly said as he passed. The constable's eyes widened.

#

An hour later Roldin, Alys, and Kinnley stood over a map of the town. Alys was scribbling frantically, her tongue sticking out of her mouth, and there was already a good-sized pile of carefully-folded parchments behind her.

"Here," she said, and showed them her schematic. "This is based on a theory I read in one of Hiribaldin's books. It's a trap that can lock itself and drop underwater. Demons can shift forms but it takes concentration, so it's hard for them to do it when in so much distress that they can't focus— Roldin also knows this to be true." The demon slayer nodded his agreement. "Their shape shifting is why regular bars or traps or binds can't hold a demon. But, if we can trap one in a cage, sort of like…no, like this one, then drop it under the floodwaters, the demon wouldn't be able to breathe, because of water and all that, and it'll eventually lose its summoning and vanish. It'll be panicking too much to change shape to slip through the bars. It's foolproof!"

Roldin shook his head. "I don't know. I've never tried to drown a demon before, but it may work." He looked up at the mayor, who shrugged.

"Your call," Kinnley said. "It would be best if we knew how many demons we're going to be dealing with."

"At least one, probably two, maybe a couple more," Roldin said. He took a sip of the warm tea in his hands and tapped his cup thoughtfully. "There's no way of knowing, but I know they have death on their minds. We just have to prepare for the worst and hope that we've imagined hard enough. Also, I think we've come up with plans to deal with just about any threat they could throw at us, from air, water, or land. What you need to do is hammer this into your people so that they know when to improvise each one as it comes. We may need only one, or two, or all. We just don't know."

"I've had to defend the town before, most recently last year when we had a slew of bandit attacks trying to take our mine," the mayor said. "We Road's End people are simple, but we'll fight if backed into a corner."

"I believe you, but I hope it doesn't come to that," Roldin said. "Demons are a little tougher to kill than a starving bandit."

"What about my water trap?" Alys asked impatiently. She was balancing on the balls of her feet in anticipation, her eyes determined behind her thick spectacles.

The demon slayer nodded. "Build it. In the meantime, I'll work with a few of the miners to take down some of the walkways, hollow out some of the abandoned houses. We'll make choke-points here, and here," he said, pointing to different places on the map, "and even a few traps, mainly as distractions. I may need to borrow your jail cell door."

The mayor nodded. "We have iron enough from the mine that was taken before this season's flooding, if you need that too. What exactly are you planning?"

"To control where they go. Demons are unpredictable with their forms, especially if you don't know who they are, but the one that is leading them I am well acquainted with. What they're really after is me, and I'll try to keep that focus on me and away from the townspeople. If we do that, this plan may just work."

"Then it's settled," Kinnley said. "I'll gather a few of the ones I trust to handle this and dole out some orders. Do you need to rest on that?" the mayor asked, pointing at Roldin's leg.

"I'll have time enough to rest on it after tomorrow, in one way or another," he said with a grin.

Kinnley shook his head. "You're a hell of a man, demon slayer. I'd like to buy you a drink tomorrow night, if we're all still here."

"Sounds like a date," Roldin said.

Aly's eyes grew large. "Aww, that's too bad. I was hoping you and Penny…"

"I — what? It's a figure of speech, Alys."

"Ooooh. Right. I've heard of those."

CHAPTER 8

FIRST AND LAST TIME

Kinnley's confidants spread the word quickly. Before noon there were dozens of townspeople out and about, doing whatever needed to be done. Several were sharpening wooden stakes from old poles, while more were retrofitting houses to whatever they were told to do. Alys was busy on one dock working on her water trap from the remains of a few of the abandoned wooden houses and an old crank-run mining elevator.

The mood of the town had changed completely in a few hours. It had come from the edge of hysteria to a steely-eyed determination to survive. Some, however, still teetered on the edge of terror, and a few had already taken as many of their things that they could carry and waded through the floodwaters and out of the town as quickly as they could. Though no one was forbidden to leave by the authorities in charge, their fellow townspeople were not as forgiving, and arguments broke out among those who wanted to stay and those who sought to escape. The mayor calmed the throng with a speech about who the real enemy was. He tried to channel their panic into preparation, and the distraction proved beneficial.

Penny and Wull toiled continuously in the tavern to feed everyone as they worked. The town's children ran around with pots of food and water. Men and women alike slogged through the midday rain at their tasks, some in stoic quiet, others doing their best to keep a sense of humor. Roldin walked among them with his crutch, answering questions and directing some of the trap makers. Each townsperson listened intently and did whatever they were told to do with great efficiency. He was amazed—he'd seen larger, better-off towns with a full garrison of guards fall into chaos when faced with such odds. The hardy people of Road's End, once over their initial shock, proved much harder to fell than Roldin would have thought.

Old Nanny cornered the demon slayer and took a look at his wounds. "And this one on your shoulder is looking better, though I'm still not sure where you got it," she chided in a grandmotherly tone.

"I'm a forty-two year old child, I guess. I always find a way to get a scrape or two."

Nanny smiled at him. "Stay off that leg if you can."

"I know, I'll try to let it heal," Roldin said seriously.

"Good. You can't go killing demons while crawling on the floor now, can you, boy?" She sauntered off and he watched her go with amazement. As she rounded a corner Linder passed her, carrying a pot of water and a ladle and offering it to workers. When he saw Roldin he paused.

Linder approached the demon slayer slowly and stopped in front of him. Roldin looked down into the boy's expressive blue eyes, eerily reminiscent of his own, and he didn't know what to do.

"Your name's not Gaeryn," Linder said.

"Ah, no," he stammered. "My name is Roldin."

"Why did you lie before?"

Roldin knelt down so he was closer to eye level with Linder, grimacing when a shot of pain went through his leg. "Because my name is dangerous. I didn't want you to be in danger, too."

The boy seemed to consider this, and looked down into the pot of water he held. "Linder, I'm sorry I yelled at you. I didn't want to hurt you."

"You didn't want to be around me."

"Because I didn't want to put you in danger," Roldin said. "It's hard to explain, but...I'm sorry. I won't do that again. I promise you."

The boy nodded sullenly, then looked around nervously. "Am I in danger now that I know your name?" he whispered.

The demon slayer swallowed back the lump in his throat. He touched the boy on the shoulder and said, "You're in no danger at all, Linder. I promise: I won't let anything happen to you."

"I believe you," his son said. Linder smiled – the innocent, trusting smile of a child – and ran back through the rain to the tavern. Roldin watched the boy go. His hand went to his axe handle and gripped it tightly until his fingers ached. He'd been in many, many fights before. This was the first time the demon slayer felt he had more to lose than just his own soul, and it brought a layer to this fight that he didn't know how to deal with. His mind whirled.

Mayor Kinnley approached with several of the miners in tow. "These are them," he told the demon slayer. "The strongest we have."

Roldin pushed away his doubts and put on a somber face. "Well, they are large," he said. The smallest of the miners made Roldin, who was a large and strong man in his own right, look childish. "But are you brave?"

"We're not warriors," one of them said.

"But we're not cowards," another chimed in.

"All I know is how to mine rocks," a third said rather sheepishly.

The demon slayer grinned wolfishly. "That's exactly what I need you to do." Then he gathered them close and discussed his plans.

Roldin realized Alys was making good headway on her trap as he continued his circuit of the town. Her tools were laid out before her on the dock and she worked tirelessly, never straying from her schematics. As he paused and watched her, two of the townspeople, one of them the town shopkeeper, walked from behind him and were speaking to each other. "Damned crazy, she is," he overheard. "Heard she was expelled from the university and didn't even realize it."

"She's an odd one, for sure. Came by my store last month once the snows melted and bought the oddest assortment of things. What does one need with a dozen hourglasses, anyway?"

"I bet she's in league with them demons," the first speculated.

"Are you both foolish?" Roldin interrupted.

The pair jumped and reeled around as one, regarding him sheepishly. "We don't mean nothing by it, demon slayer," the shopkeeper said.

"She's the only one who doesn't have to be here right now, and she's staying because she wants to help." His glare turned their faces red. "Show some respect." The two men bowed and scraped and went on their way as quickly as they dared.

Roldin continued over to Alys. "Need any help?" he asked.

She turned and grinned at him, but shook her head. "I've just about figured this out!" she said. "All I need is to reinforce this mechanism some more and we'll be set." She had modified the crank of the elevator into a release lever. The cage itself was large enough to hold six men. "Unless...should it be bigger?"

Roldin shuddered. "By the Sacreds' hoary feet, I hope not."

She bent down and smoothed out one of her crumpled schematics, studying it while chewing her bottom lip. He started to move on when Alys said quietly, "I overheard. I don't think people want me here."

Roldin grimaced. "I don't think they really believe any of that," he said. "They're scared of all this. Just has everyone on edge."

The scholar shook her head. "People always treat me like that." Her voice was softer than he'd heard before, and she spoke slower, as if through fog. "I understand why, sometimes. I know I'm kind of odd. I guess it's why I don't let myself get around people much. History is easy for me to understand — it already happened. What's done is done and it can be quantified, analyzed. But with people, and the present...I just don't know how to deal with the unknown. I don't really have much in common with them."

The demon slayer put his arms over the railing of the dock, stretching his leg out and thought for a minute. "Saeralyx told me once that it feels that way, sometimes, in the demon home realm. Its interests are so different from the other demons that Saer is pretty much an outcast. Its ideas, and approach to our world in general, are regarded as heresy by many."

"Saeralyx seems pretty amazing to me," Alys laughed.

"Yes," Roldin agreed. "Saeralyx operates on another level from the other demons, just like you do from people. You're smarter than them, and they don't quite appreciate your mind. Take it from me: people fear what they don't understand."

"They're afraid of me? Me. Hah, I wouldn't hurt a mouse!" Her exuberance returned along with the striking grin on her face. "In fact, when I was a child I adopted all the mice on my block and put them all together in a box. They had little mouse houses, with little mouse beds, and I made them food and brought them other mice to play with. My mother just didn't understand why more was merrier!"

Roldin nodded reluctantly. "That could be a… bad example, but your heart was in the right place."

She nodded at him, her water-logged spectacles making her eyes shimmer.

He saw Jodas lead a handcart through the plankways, doling out weapons to citizens. It was loaded with older swords, mostly useless pickaxes, and hastily thrown together spears. "It's amazing to me that a mining town doesn't have a blacksmith," Roldin commented.

"We can't get one to stay," the constable lamented. "Damned flood waters and the promise of two seasons without visiting customers always sends them packing. This is what we have, though."

Roldin nodded. "It'll have to do."

"I know we don't have any of your moon-iron forged weapons, to really get into a demon's hide. Believe me, if I had a spear like that no demon would dare set foot in this town." The constable pushed out his chest and tried to suck in his stomach. His mail bulged in all the wrong places.

Roldin coughed to hide the grin that threatened to spread on his face and looked down, then patted the dark axe at his side. "It helps, but any determined fighter can pierce a demon's defenses." The demon slayer reached out and gripped the constable by the upper arm, then raised his eyebrows. "Especially one as strong as you! Don't fret about these weapons. The real strength is in the person who wields it."

Jodas beamed, trying his best to hide it. Roldin continued his walk around the town. By mid-afternoon his leg was screaming at him. He found his way to the tavern, where Penny and Wull were still running around to prepare food for everyone. The demon slayer approached the bar. "Can I trouble you for some water, and a washbasin?"

"Now you're askin' for water. Want a foot rub next, your highness?" Penny said exasperated, but with a grin.

"Well, if it wouldn't be too much trouble…"

"Don't push my goodwill, demon slayer. I don't have much to pass around." She handed over the requested items and continued her preparations.

Roldin sat down in a chair, hard, and sighed in pleasure as he set his crutch aside and rubbed his injured leg. He drank deeply of the water, then poured the rest in the washbasin. He took out four empty glass vials from his pack and set them on the table, then removed his axe and a whetstone. Leaning over the basin, he sharpened the axe, letting specks of black metal fall into the water.

Penny rushed by him, then saw what he was doing, and stopped. "What in the hells are you up to?"

Roldin laughed. "Do you remember the vial I used in my fight with Zhanny, the one I smashed into its chest?" Penny nodded in recollection. "This is what's in there. Something about this metal hurts them, either as a weapon or even as dust in the water. This is like scalding water on their skin."

Penny's eyebrows went up. "I wish that worked on anybody. I have a few people I'd like to scald on a whim." She glanced at Wull, who looked up from the stove and finally noticed Roldin there.

"Oh, demon slayer," he said nervously. "I, uh didn't see…no hard feelings, right?"

"No hard feelings," Roldin replied. The portly barkeep nodded and smiled. "I'll just let them kill you first…" Roldin muttered under his breath.

"What was that?" Penny asked with an arched eyebrow.

"Nothing, we're not all going to die and I'm not going to allow Wull to get flayed alive first and laugh at his screams of anguish—that would be silly." The barmaid snorted a laugh and headed back to the bar. Roldin stopped her with a tug on her sleeve. "Has Jodas been by here yet? Do you have anything to defend yourself with?"

She rolled her eyes. "I'd use the golden pick behind the bar again but when Wull found out what I'd done with it the other night he grew pale as a ghost and hid it under his bed. Instead Jodas brought me the world's nubbiest mining pick. I swear it was wielded by the first idiot who ever cracked a rock. I think I'd feel safer armed with my rolling pin."

Roldin reached behind his back and brought out his dagger, sheath and belt. "Here, keep this on you," he said, and handed it to her. "It's probably more useful than a rolling pin."

Penny took it and unsheathed it. The silver metal gleamed at her, flawless and sharp as a razor. "Thank you," she said rather breathlessly. "It's beautiful."

"It's stubborn, is what it is, but it will protect you well." Roldin said and shook his head. "You know, I've tried to break that dagger several times over the years. I've abused it, dishonored it by cleaning my fingernails with it, and left it out in the rain. I've stabbed things with it that should have broken it and the damn thing still stays in one piece."

"Sounds like a pretty good dagger, to me."

"I suppose…my father gave it to me," Roldin said. He was quiet for a moment. "It was the first and last time he ever gave me anything. I've held onto it since that day, in case I ever see him again."

"And what happens when that day comes?"

"Then I give it back to him," Roldin said darkly.

THIRTY TWO YEARS EARLIER

The boy traversed the dark streets of Neppeth, not walking so much as hopping from shadow to shadow. A cold snap had come from the north and Roldin knew being outside the walls, especially without a fire, would be deadly. The night before he'd woken up with numb toes after another one of his nightmares and the day had grown more frigid from there, so he'd made the rare decision to enter the town. Just being inside – with its many walls and surrounded by buildings wherever he went –had him on edge.

The guards largely left him alone, though from time to time one of the patrolmen would glance at him a bit too long. When that happened, he would speed to an alleyway and hide for a few moments before emerging to continue in an opposite direction. As uncomfortable as the walls made him, at least he wasn't freezing to death. He was too unnerved to sleep, so he had vowed to spend the night walking the roads, stopping at braziers here and there for a few moments of warmth. That way, if he felt the Dread grip him, he could just keep running. His evolving route to the town gate was always at the forefront of his mind.

He turned down a largely empty market street, well-lit with lamps. The stores were all closed. Roldin looked through the storefronts displaying clothes and food. He once again mulled over the thought of burglary, but he wouldn't know the first way to go about that. He tried to think back to the books he'd read but he didn't believe any of them would be very helpful. As he eyed a particularly warm-looking coat, he caught his reflection in a storefront window and couldn't believe what he was looking at.

Some creature of the wilds stared back at him. His hair was tangled and knotted from being barely washed in cold forest streams for weeks. His clothes were ripped in places; one ragged sleeve ended halfway down his forearm. As torn as his clothes were, they seemed to engulf his tiny frame. His face looked sunken, his eyes dark-rimmed and hollow, and his cloak hung from bony shoulders like a shroud. No wonder some of the guards had looked at him oddly.

Roldin was suddenly very conscious of his appearance. He tried to rub his hair down with his hands. His father had never really cared what the boy looked like but he'd at least insisted on looking friendly enough to sell things to potential buyers, and if he were here he'd no doubt beat a better pair of pants onto his son.

"But you're not here," he said out loud, fiercely, and jumped at the sound of his own voice. It was hoarse and cracked and thick with sudden use, but odder to him was the tone of it. There was something menacing in that tone...dangerous. Roldin had never thought of himself as dangerous. The boy stared at the hungry stranger for a few moments more. It didn't make sense...none of it made sense.

Movement from the side caught his eye. Two men wandered onto the main market street, conversing together in hushed tones. Roldin turned and started off, not too quickly, ducking into an alleyway.

His eyes took a moment to adjust after the relative brightness of the main street. His foot slipped into a puddle of something in the dark and the splash echoed off of the stone walls surrounding him. The boy found a crate and shrunk behind it, holding his knees close, and waited for the men to pass. He took some comfort in the darkness of the alleyway and risked a look at his surroundings.

The two men stopped at the mouth of the alley. Roldin held his breath. One pointed into the darkness and the two of them entered, shuffling slowly through. The boy, as quietly as he could, reached for his father's dagger. He unlatched it from its *sheath and slowly drew it. His palms were already sweating.*

He didn't know what he was prepared to do with it. The dagger felt odd in his hands, like it didn't belong. Roldin didn't have time to consider any more as the two men drew closer to his hiding spot. They were whispering again but the boy didn't understand anything that was said. When one of the men found the same puddle, his splash loud and intrusive in the night, the boy took off from his hiding place and did the one thing he knew he was good at.

The men barked something behind him but his footsteps drowned out whatever it was. He focused on the other end of the alleyway, watching the bright opening get closer, and was already planning which direction he would go next. Just as he reached the street a figure appeared before him, a dark mass against the light ahead. Strong hands gripped him by the shoulders.

The boy didn't scream — his heart was too tired for any of that — but he did twist against the grip. He was held fast. Almost too late he remembered the dagger. With a movement borne of desperation he lunged out with it, only to have his thin arm grabbed by one of the men behind him.

"Easy lad, easy!" one of them said. Roldin continued to struggle but didn't dignify whatever they wanted by showing any fear. His father's dagger was wrenched from his hand, and the man who held it walked around in front of him. "You're going to hurt yourself with this," he chided.

Roldin snarled. He didn't know where the sound had come from and it surprised him more than the men around him. They looked at him thoughtfully. "Think this is him?" one asked another.

"Could be," said one.

The man holding him by the shoulders sighed. "You stupid louts, just ask him," he said, and turned the skinny boy around with an effortless spin. The grip on his arms was tight but not overly cruel. "Lad, is your name Roldin?"

The boy paused entirely. His whole body stiffened. Three men were looking at him expectantly and he had no idea what that meant.

"Are you Roldin?" the man repeated.

He didn't know what the answer should be. At that moment his stomach sank and he was afraid he would be sick. His body, rigid with constant alertness, began to sag from exhaustion. The last few weeks of strain and flight reared its head all at once, and it was more than the child could bear. Tears came to his eyes and his body shook with sobs. He found himself nodding his head before he'd finish deciding what he was going to do.

They took him to a nearby tavern and sat him down in the back, away from curious customers who wondered what kind of sewer the child had been plucked from. Warm tea was placed in his hands. He took it numbly, instantly warmed by it, not caring that it burned his tongue in a most beautiful and wonderfully painful way. He was given food, too — bread, and meat, and vegetables that weren't raw and cold from the chilly ground. The sight of food in front of him dulled any worry he had about his situation and he ate quickly.

"We've been looking for you a long time," said one of them. He was young, his head shaved, his grin friendly and gap-toothed. "We've been all through this town and the woods around here for days." The man put a hand over Roldin's shoulder and squeezed. The boy straightened a little under the touch and looked at the arm warily — the hint of an intricate tattoo barely peeked out from underneath the sleeve. The shoulder still hurt where one of the other men had gripped him. "You don't have to be afraid anymore. We'll protect you now."

The boy let his mouth drop open in a gape, and then a slow smile crept across his face. He was afraid his tears would return. He didn't trust them, but they said they would protect him, and he wondered for a moment if his nightmare had ended. The words were something that his ears had desperately needed to hear.

"Your father sent us to find you, son," one of the men, an older one with a drooping grey mustache, said reassuringly.

"He's very worried about you," the bald man said with a nod. "Sorry about what he'd done. He wants to see you safe."

"We'll take you to him tomorrow," the third said. He didn't smile, though. His eyes were bright grey and caught the light of the nearby tavern's fire like a wolf's.

Roldin didn't let his smile falter. Inside, though, something as strong as the Dread gripped his heart and held on tight. The boy had to admit that the feeling of hopelessness was somehow reassuring and welcoming after he had abandoned it — for a moment, not being afraid had made him feel naked and exposed. The inside of his mind screamed in warning so loudly that he was worried the three men would somehow hear it. He imagined that his hackles rose.

"That's wonderful," he said, forcing himself to smile wider. The strain made his back start to sweat. "I've been so tired…"

"Ah, of course," the mustachioed man said with a smile. "I'll take you to your room where you can get a good night's rest."

Roldin let himself be led up some stairs and down a dark, wooden hallway. The only light came from a small candle set on a console table. The man took it and held it up to lead the rest of the way to a small room at the end. "Here you are. We'll be just next door. Bang on the wall if you need anything."

"Can I…" the boy started, then looked down sheepishly.

The man bent down and got eye level with him, his smile toothy. "What do you want?"

"Can I have my dagger back?" he said. "It's my father's, and it's all I've had for a while. I want to keep it so I can give it back to him tomorrow."

Roldin could see the wheels turning in the man's mind. Ultimately he shrugged and slipped the dagger from his belt and handed it to the boy. "Whatever makes you feel better," he said. "Now get some sleep — we'll leave before dawn."

With that the man shut the door. Roldin didn't move, but stood there and watched the door silently. After a few moments he could hear the sound of a key slowly making its way into the lock, and then a heavy click. There was no latch on the inside of the door. He and his father had stayed at taverns like this many times, and the rooms were meant to make it easier for crooked innkeepers to come in and take your valuables in the night rather than letting you keep them secured. The boy knew he was locked in.

He turned and looked around the room. It was lit by a stubby candle, illuminating a bed, a tall wooden closet, a weak-looking chest, and a single window. He walked over to the glass and pulled — it was lacquered shut. Weeks of being on the run had done a lot to curb his outward panic, and instead of losing himself he calmly began feeling along the edge of the glass pane for any seams he could take advantage of. It was sealed well. Breaking it would be too loud and out of the question, and he also thought he was somewhere on the third floor of the inn.

The boy sat on the bed and continued to ponder his options. He eyed the walls, specifically. They felt alien to him after so long in the forest. They seemed to be getting closer. Despite his best efforts panic was taking hold of him. His breaths came fast. He avoided the walls and looked up at the ceiling. It was made of wooden boards, much like the floor. There was a knothole in one of them that was black against the bare light of the candle. He felt like it was watching him, like the eyes in his nightmares did, cold and sinister.

He knew they had no intentions of taking him to his father. His father was long gone by now, bathing in the coin he had received for what had been done to him. Whatever these men had in store for him was not good. All his running the past few weeks had been for nothing. The sorrow around his heart tugged at him as strongly as that thing had done, all those nights ago.

His father's dagger was in his hand. Roldin looked at it. It was beautiful — his father's prized possession. The boy touched the point with a finger, watched as it bit into his flesh, ever so slightly. Blood bloomed dully in the candlelight, as present as the oozing wound on his palm.

"I'll finish it," he whispered to himself. Roldin imagined pushing the dagger into his chest the way he had just cut his finger. "I'll finish what you started, father." They wanted him alive or he'd be dead now, he knew. He could rob them of their prize. He went as far as holding the dagger to himself with both hands before he realized he couldn't do it. His hands shook and he let the dagger drop to the bed. He buried his face in his hands and tried to keep himself from screaming.

He heard footsteps, heavy, coming near his room, and hushed voices outside his door. Roldin sat very still. Moments later, the footsteps moved away and he heard a door open down the hall. As it shut, the room shook. The walls were thin enough that he could hear the men's voices on the other side.

Roldin looked up at the ceiling again, searching for another way. He stared at the knothole.

As quietly as he could he lifted the chest and placed it near the wooden closet. He took off his shoes so his footsteps would be quieter, then stood on top of the chest, which easily supported his weight. He sucked on his bleeding finger, then gripped the top of the closet and pulled himself up. It rocked slightly, knocking against the floor. He froze until it stopped, then continued. Roldin climbed on top and then turned over, lying on his back where he could easily reach the ceiling. He took the dagger and found the knothole and worked his way around it along the seam of the wooden plank. Dust and splinters fell in his face. He persisted.

Rain began to fall outside, heavy and thudding against the window, and it sounded like it was more ice than water. He could still hear the men's voices next door, an oddly constant chatter. The vicious point of the dagger easily fit in the seam of the wood and, though it was noisy, he worked on loosening the board. It finally came loose and nearly dropped on top of him, but the boy caught it, barely. Out of breath, he put the board next to him on top of the closet and judged the size of the opening. He could fit.

Afraid to wait any longer, Roldin climbed up through the ceiling and above his room. There was a small window far off, part of some attic that was no longer used, and through the light that shone from the street he could make out rafters that he could crawl on. He also saw a leak in the roof, where rain had already begun to seep through. A rusted bucket had been placed below it.

The boy paused – it was beyond the men's room, but it was his only choice. He sheathed the dagger and crawled up on the rafter, praying to all the Sacreds he could think of that he wouldn't make any noise. Even so, the boards creaked under his meager weight. Instead of crawling he scooted himself slowly along the rafter, as fast as he dared. His hands found spider webs that he brushed away in the darkness. Dust threatened to invade his lungs at every breath.

Roldin knew he was above the men's room. He could still hear the voices. They were speaking in rhythmic tones, like chanting. Were they singing? He couldn't tell. The boy did his best to ignore it and kept going.

There was a light ahead of him, coming from below. A knothole was there, similar to the one in his own room, and candlelight seeped its way up to him. The dust he disturbed as he made his way swirled in the small beam of light like smoke. He was almost over the knothole when he could hear the men more clearly. They were indeed chanting, and as much as he knew he had to move... he stopped, put his eye to the hole, and looked through.

Two of the men sat on the beds, bare-chested, knives in their hands. They had cut themselves along their tattoos on their forearms, like the one he had seen earlier on the third man, and were dripping blood onto what looked like stones sitting on top of white cloths. The blood bloomed red and dark around each rock.

Roldin didn't understand what he was seeing. He watched, fascinated, and also a little horrified at the sight. As he studied the men cutting themselves, and all the blood...he was glad he had not decided to go through with it earlier, as he couldn't fathom what it would be like doing that to himself. He'd had enough. Whatever was going on, he wanted no part of and he sat up to keep moving along the rafter. He could see the leak on the roof and his way out, only feet away.

His stomach suddenly cramped. He heard something, quiet, in the back of his head. A ringing, but it was barely there. So faint...

He spared another glance below and had to blink twice at what he was seeing. The stones on the bed began to shimmer. Black smoke began to rise from nothing, forming a shadow that began to engulf the room.

The Dread came back to him, clear, but still faint. Roldin didn't understand but he unquestionably knew what it meant. No longer caring for slow stealth, he hurried along the rafter, slipping and hitting the boards below him as he did. The boom made him wince, but desperation had set in. He heard a single deep voice below him shout in alarm, then the sound of footsteps as one of them rushed towards Roldin's room

The boy made it to the leak and stabbed at it with his dagger, then tore at it with his hands. Rotten shingles fell away easily, and rain poured into the hole. Roldin emerged from the opening, shocked by the sudden chill of the rain and sleet, and crawled barefoot onto the roof. The Dread leapt from the back of his head to the forefront of his mind, as loud as being inside a ringing temple bell.

Through the rainy darkness he could see where the roof sloped into another building, then step down above a balcony in a house next door. Ignoring all lingering pretense of stealth, he ran, his feet already numbed by the freezing rain, and let himself slip and slide off the tavern roof onto the balcony below. He risked a look back as he did and saw something emerge from the hole he had crawled out of –something big and black against the *cloudy sky.*

Roldin fell onto the balcony with a thud and slid several feet before he came to a stop. He looked down and could see a cart being hastily loaded with bags by several men who hurried through their work against the rain. The boy jumped and hit the bags with another thud. Luckily whatever was in them was soft.

The men voiced their disapproval but he was already on the move. A shriek went up behind him, and all the men's faces turned toward the sound. Roldin kept running.

The streets were even emptier now. His only company was the sound of his bare feet on the cobblestone streets and the icy rain that fell relentlessly around him. Behind him the shriek repeated itself. He thought it sounded furious.

Roldin gripped the dagger, sheathed on his belt, hard. "Never again," he panted to himself as he ran.

CHAPTER 9

WITH THESE HANDS

Night fell on Road's End. The town looked nothing like it had a day before. Half of the walkways were dismantled, stopped suddenly, or took odd, nonsensical turns. There were gaps in the rows of houses where abandoned ones had been taken down or gutted for scrap. Some of the walkways had sharpened stakes sticking out at all angles, and in the front of the town, where the road forked, an entire palisade was erected from the waters, closing off the town.

The normally docile plankways were patrolled by guards who had a set route through the three-forked town. These citizens had a mismatched set of armor that had been thrown together at the last minute, made mostly from pieces of leather clothing and old boots. There was a curfew that the mayor had announced for most of the townsfolk, for safety. Torches were erected in the normally dark town, leaving almost no corner unlit. Demons' promise of arriving tomorrow or not, Roldin didn't wish to take any chances on an early surprise attack. Preparations had been made and the townspeople all knew their places to take for the battle—all that was left was to wait.

The guards watched as Penny, Alys, and Roldin walked the town. The demon slayer observed the various traps, paths, and ambush points that had been setup, and he was impressed. "They did a lot today," he said.

"I barely recognize it," Penny said sadly. "I know it's necessary, but now the town feels like one of King Twill's strongholds. They make you feel guilty just for stepping foot there. The guards' leers make it worse."

"Whoa," Alys yelled behind them.

Penny and Roldin turned to her and the young woman was teetering on one foot, shaking her head vigorously and hitting herself with the heel of her hand. Penny's head tilted to one side. "Alys, you alright?"

"Well, it's the oddest thing," she said, hopping around on one foot. "There's something in my head and I just can't get it out."

"Something doing…what?"

"It's talking to me! It sounds like…"

Roldin nodded. "Saeralyx," he said. Both women looked at him. "It's one of the aftereffects of a summoning. For a few days afterwards the demon is able to talk to you from their realm—something about it being through your blood and all."

"This is so bizarre," Alys said as she continued contorting. "Does it want something? Maybe to be summoned again?"

"Maybe," the demon slayer said. "But don't do it."

"Why not?" Penny asked. "Maybe Saeralyx could help us fight?"

"That's precisely what I don't want," Roldin said seriously. "Saeralyx would defend me in a heartbeat, but the torture and punishment it would receive at the hands of other demons in its own realm is…unfathomable. I won't be the cause of that."

Penny nodded an agreement, and Roldin looked hard at Alys until she did the same. She shook her head one last time and made herself dizzy.

"Is anyone hungry?" Penny asked. "I've been cooking all day but I don't think I ate anything."

Roldin said, "I'm hungry, too, but I'll cook. You should sit down." Penny and Alys both gave him skeptical glances. "What, you think I can't cook? I'm alone in the wilderness most of the time. I don't just eat berries all day. I have to know how to make edible food or else I'd starve to death from boredom."

They dined in Penny's house. Linder sat at the kitchen table and pretended not to listen as the three of them discussed various details about the coming battle while Roldin prepared the meal.

"Is your trap ready to go?" he asked Alys.

"As ready as it'll ever be," she smiled. "Wait until Hiribaldin hears how well it works! Or, at least he would hear about it if he were still living. Who knows, it may work so well that maybe he'll hear about it anyway!"

Roldin nodded seriously and struggled to hide his smile. "You've studied demons for years, right?" She nodded at him, her wild tangle of hair flying. "Did you ever think you'd fight them?"

"No, not really," she said thoughtfully. "I'm not really the violent type, but..." she grabbed a piece of carrot that Roldin was chopping and played with it in her fingers. "I think I always wanted to learn more about them because they scared me so. Figured if I learned all I could, I would know how to avoid them, how to protect myself. I suppose I always thought this day would come." She shook her head and giggled suddenly. "There I go, being all dark and gloomy."

Penny snorted. "Well, if there was ever a time that gloomy would be appropriate..." she said, then put a comforting hand on Linder's head. Her son smiled at her. "Why don't you go read your book?" she prompted, and the boy rolled his eyes but complied. She watched him go and turned back with a sigh. "But let's not talk about that now."

"Right!" Alys grinned. "Let's guess how bad Roldin's cooking is going to be."

The demon slayer shrugged at them. "What did I do to earn this ire?"

Both women rested their chins on their hands. Penny grinned and narrowed her eyes. "It's just amusing how domestic the mighty 'Gaeryn Blackthorn' is when he's not wooing women with lies and his pretty eyes."

Roldin grinned as he put some vegetables into a cooking pot. "Pretty eyes, is it?" he asked without looking up, so he couldn't see her blush. Alys giggled enough that Penny silenced her with a hard punch in the arm.

He went back to chopping more vegetables as Penny began to rub her feet. Alys studied his chopping motions intensely. "What?" Roldin asked with a raised eyebrow when he noticed her peculiar expression.

"I was just mulling over the effectiveness of your knife there. You're more comfortable with the axe...could that be used to chop vegetables with more efficiency? Is it clean enough to be used for that purpose? You figure you'd need to consider size, velocity... "

"No."

"But—"

"No," Roldin repeated, pointing his kitchen knife at her. "Besides, I paid too much coin for that to use it to prepare dinner with."

The scholar turned to the axe, leaning near the door, and considered it for a moment. "With that much moon-iron, I'd expect so. Where did you get it?"

Roldin shrugged. "Nowhere special. Most demon slayers worth their salt try to carry something made of it on them, at least a dagger or an arrowhead. I'm…busier than most demon slayers, so I made it a point to take every advantage I could. I spent two months in the northern badlands looking for a crater that hadn't been picked through yet to find enough of it for that axe. Then I took it to a smith who forged it for me, for a hefty sum. Moon-iron is hard to work with."

Alys looked a bit crestfallen. "Oh, I thought there'd be more of a story to it, like you found it in the lair of a dragon!"

"Dragons don't exist," he muttered.

"Aww."

Roldin finished stirring his stew and dipped a spoon in for a perfunctory taste. "Well now," he said with a growing grin, "I dare you to find fault with this."

Linder came back into the kitchen and watched as Penny reached into the pot with her own spoon without taking her doubtful look away from the demon slayer, and tried it as well. Alys followed suit as Penny chewed in thought. "Very well, it's a tasty stew," she said with a sigh. "Could use some more seasoning, though," Penny said softly. This time it was Roldin's turn to throw a glob of dough at Penny. Linder went into a giggle fit as the demon slayer and the bar maid bickered on the other side of the kitchen.

Alys picked up the dough and started shaping it with her hands. "Such a silly choice for a weapon," she said quietly to herself. "This current shape is not conducive to achieving maximum dough-tossing velocity or harm of any kind."

Linder looked at her funny, and Alys turned red and put the dough down quickly. The boy picked it up, continuing her adjustments, and presented it to her with a nod. She took it as if she were being handed a great prize, hefted it, weighed it, and examined it from all angles. "You're some kind of genius child," she said to Linder in awe. Then she took aim and threw it at Penny. It hit her square in the back of the head, and the barmaid whirled.

"She did it!" the boy screamed.

"He designed it!" she argued.

Penny made a face, then turned and punched Roldin in the arm.

"Hey, why—?"

"Because you started it."

Roldin began to argue, then thought better of it.

They ate around the kitchen table, mostly in silence. Every so often Roldin would look outside through the rain at the many torches that lit Road's End, a crease of worry growing around the corners of his mouth. Alys noticed and put a hand on his back, bringing the man's attention back to the table.

"Eat," she urged. "There'll be time for worry later."

He laughed and nodded reluctantly. He finished his stew and sat back, resting his hands over his stomach and smiling. "Well don't you look pleased with yourself," Penny said and rolled her eyes.

"I know a good meal when I eat one," he said with a contented sigh. Linder laughed and Penny shook her head. The demon slayer stopped mid-smile, a troubling thought worming its way somewhere in the back of his mind. He couldn't tell what it was, but it caused him to look around, trying to figure out whatever was troubling him. Penny and Linder started talking about books but Roldin only half-listened, restlessness beginning to creep in.

It wasn't until later, as the four of them sat near the fire in the main room and Alys was telling them about a lecture she'd attended on the theory of the origins of laughing and Linder and Penny listened while putting all of the strange theories she recited from memory to task, that Roldin realized what it was. He swept his eyes around the room again, taking in the cozy fireplace, the overstuffed bookshelves, the comfortable cushions he was sitting on, the colorful drawings on the wall, and his son sitting there laughing and smiling ear-to-ear, and realized the unease he was feeling was that he *wasn't* uneasy. He rubbed the back of his neck and smiled, shook his head, and turned his attention to the people around him.

There was no way he was going to miss any of this.

Their conversation was broken at times by long stretches of comfortable silence. Penny and Roldin got into a playfully heated debate about the best wine that would have gone with the stew, if there had been any more in the town to drink. Alys started teaching Linder words for things like fire and destruction in the demon language, also taking a piece of parchment and teaching him how to write it. Penny finally looked over at the scholar with wide eyes and chided sternly but quietly, "Alys, don't teach my son demonic."

The younger woman began to argue the relative safety of learning it as Linder's attention turned elsewhere. The boy wandered around the room, then found himself in front of Roldin's axe, sitting near the door. He picked it up, straining to lift the weight, and admired the weapon with a smile.

Roldin noticed with a start. His breath caught in his

throat at the sight. He got up and very gently took the axe from the boy's hands. "It's not a toy, you should be careful," he said with a shallow smile, trying not to alarm him.

"I know what it is," Linder said, sticking his chin out. "Do you think I'd ever be big and strong enough to use something like that?"

The demon slayer turned away and placed the axe next to the door again. "I hope, with all my heart, that you'll never have to."

The boy looked at him oddly. "Why not?"

Roldin smiled softly, his eyes shining in the firelight. He fought against the breaking of his voice. "Because you should have books in your hands instead. You...you should spend your days in a cozy chair reading a good story, having a good meal, and then spending all night talking with the people you love until your throat is sore but you don't care because you're so happy that you could burst. You should have the time to think of all the things you want to do and then have the will to do them, and love as hard as you can as often as you can." He gripped the boy's hands in his own. "Because creating and learning and dreaming with these hands is so much more meaningful than destroying."

"But, I want to protect people, like you."

"It can be a noble thing," he said reluctantly, "but it takes something out of you." The warrior put a tender hand on Linder's chest. "Keep it all in here. Keep it all in here for as long as you can."

His son looked at him quizzically. Roldin laughed and stood, wiping his eyes quickly. "You'll understand, one day," he said and tousled the boy's hair.

Penny was watching them, her expression

unreadable.

The night wore on and they traded stories of better days. Other times they just sat there together, listening to the rain on the rooftop, lost in their own thoughts about tomorrow. Linder fell asleep nestled between Roldin and Penny. The woman gently stroked her son's hair. "To be young and carefree again," she mused with a smile.

"I don't think youth is a requirement," Roldin said, and nodded to Alys, who was snoring softly lying on one of the cushions, her head resting on a strategically placed tangle of her hair.

Penny laughed softly, then shook her head. "I don't know how they do it. I can't see myself sleeping at all tonight, with what's coming tomorrow." She turned her gaze outside the window at the dark and quiet town. "How can it be so calm out there before...."

The demon slayer closed his eyes. "There's only so much a mind can handle. I've had many nights like this, and while they don't get any easier you just learn to cope." He shrugged and fussed with a loose thread at the end of his tunic. "I remember once, years ago, I was tracking some cultists in the mountains on the west side of Adren. I knew the only pass they could be coming out and I waited for them for days and days. It was me alone against a dozen, but I didn't want whatever demon they were in there summoning to make it out. Even with days of preparation my odds of survival were slim and all I had for company were my thoughts and worries. But I didn't go mad, because instead of looking at what's coming you just have to live in the present. Worrying will not make the future come faster. Sometimes your mind can only handle the now."

"And how are you handling the now?"

"Much better than I expected," he admitted with a

laugh. Roldin looked down at Linder.

Penny's eyebrows furrowed; her voice turned serious. "He should never know."

He nodded. "I agree. It wouldn't serve any purpose."

"But you want him to know."

"I…only so he doesn't make the same mistakes I did. I don't want him to…" and then he exhaled vigorously and shook his head quickly and began again. "He can't grow up to be me. Don't let him go through life with a weapon in his hand." Roldin looked at Penny, and she him, and the two left the rest of their personal wishes for their child unspoken.

Alys stirred in her sleep, shook her head, and looked sleepily at the two of them. "Blargh," she muttered, then she fought to stand up and said, "The mayor found me an empty house to sleep in. I may need to get a few winks, I suppose."

Penny sighed. "Good luck with that."

"Battle tomorrow…yaaay," she mock-cheered softly, and both Roldin and Penny raised their eyebrows at her. She coughed and adjusted her mess of hair and waved half-heartedly as she stepped out into the rainy night.

Penny stood up and stretched. "I've got to get him to bed, then I need to get back to the tavern, help Wull finish preparations for tomorrow."

Roldin said, "You go ahead, I'll put him to bed."

Penny paused. "Are you sure?"

"Please?" he asked.

The barmaid laughed. "Alright, but watch out if you wake him up. He turns into a little chatterbox when tired."

Roldin shrugged. "That's fine with me."

Penny left and the demon slayer carefully picked Linder up off the cushion and carried him into the tiny bedroom off of the main room. The space was cluttered with books, some toys, and drawings. The boy stirred as he was tucked into bed.

"Roldin, are you scared?"

The man nodded his head. "It's hard not to be. We don't know a lot about what will happen tomorrow."

"Do you think we'll win?"

He laughed. "I hope so."

"I finished the book," Linder said with a frown. "The ending was sad."

The demon slayer's face was puzzled. "You thought so? I don't remember it being sad. The hero finishes storming the dungeon and defeats his mortal enemy. Then he rides off into the sunset! It's a classic."

"But he's all alone."

Roldin smiled. "He's not completely alone," he said as he adjusted the blanket around Linder's neck. "He knows his mother and father love him back at his castle, and he knows the woman that he fell in love with also loves him back. He has a job to do and a journey to make, but he knows that there are people who want to see him again. Not everyone who is alone feels lonely. Sometimes they…just have somewhere to go."

The boy pondered that idea. He continued to do so until he fell asleep. Roldin watched him for a while, taking in the smell of the room, the colors on the wall as the candlelight danced on its edges. The wind blew outside and rain fell loudly against the window for a moment. Linder twitched in his sleep, a small motion that ruffled the sheets around his neck. His face contorted in some kind of dream. The demon slayer shivered sympathetically as he watched the boy snuggle down further in his already deep slumber. Roldin was amazed at how small the boy was, how fragile. *Was I ever that delicate?* he thought to himself.

He had to force himself to get up and leave.

THIRTY TWO YEARS EARLIER

Roldin was woken from another impossibly dark dream by his shivering. As much as he felt relief at no longer being held by a dozen clawed hands, the cold and dark and stabbing hunger around him was no more welcome. The boy sat up and looked around at the dark forest, eyes bleary and half-open, and stopped as he saw the flicker of firelight twinkling further out into the woods, away from the town.

He could do nothing but stare at the unexpected sight for many moments. That light could be anything. It could mean warmth or it could mean death, and he had to stop and gauge how desperate he was. Curiosity and fatigue got the better of him, and the boy shakily stood and made his way as silently as he could toward the orange glow that beckoned him through the cold, dark woods.

There was a single man. He was old, with more grey than black in his tightly-bound ponytail and unkempt beard. He had a pack beside him and a bedroll spread out on the ground. He was cooking a couple of rabbits over the fire, and there was a bow and quiver of arrows leaning next to him on the tree, though it was outside his current reach. The old man looked strong, and he wore a simple leather jerkin and good boots. Roldin couldn't figure out what the man was even doing out here. He could see his tree stump on the other side of the man's camp. It didn't seem as if his cache had been discovered. Rotten luck, he thought, that this man had picked here to camp.

The smell of the cooking meat was nearly intoxicating. Roldin gripped the dagger in his waistband, the memory of the men who had tried to take him in Neppeth vivid in his mind. Logic told him to stay away, but...he licked his lips as he weighed his options, and he also looked down at his shoeless feet. He was lucky that the weather had warmed, but even so he knew he needed a change in fortune, and fast. "You should come out," the old man suddenly called. "I can hear you out there. May as well stay closer to the fire." It was like being chided by an elder. It wasn't threatening, not really, but authoritative.

Roldin poised to run, but then he had a thought. It wasn't a particularly noble thought, but he was growing weaker by the day, and he was beginning to get desperate for any kind of relief. He steeled himself with a mantra: this fool comes to my forest and makes camp near my stump; let's see how he likes my friends.

The boy stepped out sheepishly, wrapping himself tighter in his cloak. It was the first time he'd seen a fire in a long time and he felt very exposed being lit like that out in the open. The old man raised an eyebrow at him. "Well, boy, you look like you've had a rough time," he said with a chuckle. "No sense in wasting both these rabbits on myself. Come, have a seat."

Roldin did as he was told, feigning hesitancy. In reality the rabbit looked so good that he wouldn't mind if it was poisoned. The old man also had a kettle on the fire, poured hot tea in a cup and handed it to him. He took it and sipped slowly.

"Some dangerous things about this forest," the man said while tending to the roasting food. "Why are you out here?" He took out a tin plate, placed some of the meat on it, and handed it to Roldin.

The boy bit into a rabbit haunch. The hot grease fell over his chin but he didn't care, and he attacked the rest ravenously. "I could ask you the same."

The man chuckled. "Fair enough. I'm a hunter. Came looking for game," he said with a shrug.

"I'm a forager," Roldin said. That seemed to satisfy the old man.

They ate together for a time. Roldin finished his rabbit after licking the bones clean. It was an odd feeling, to have a warm belly again. It seemed to waken civilized niceties that he'd held buried since he'd turned to thieving and spending his time in the forest outside city walls. He reached into his cloak and took out a piece of bread he had stolen last time he had been in Neppeth, ripped it in half, and offered some to the old man.

"Mighty kind of you," the man said, and took the bread with a nod. "Name's Varcus."

"My name is – " he began, then remembered the other night. He paled for a moment, then took a large bite of the bread to unconvincingly hide his hesitation. "Gaeryn."

"Good to know you," said the old man.

Roldin stared at the fire until his eyes couldn't make out the darkness beyond it anymore, though he kept himself aware of whatever the man was doing. Varcus leaned over and poked it fresh. As he did so, the Dread came back to the boy, sudden and fierce, screaming into his ears once again. It was so strong that his leg jerked on impulse. The old man didn't seem to notice.

This man had been nice to him, but Roldin had developed a plan, and his survival instincts urged him to stick to it. He would let these creatures come for him. When they did, if this man was as stupid and honorable as he seemed, he'd maybe use that bow to defend him. Then Roldin would have time to run, with a full belly and his hiding places undiscovered – though he may have to find a new hollow stump the next day. And maybe the creature would leave some of the old man's supplies behind. Roldin could figure out how to shoot with a bow...

The silent screams in his head grew louder. He leaned in closer to the fire, pretending to warm his hands, but he was trying to make himself as small as possible. Another sound, real this time, came from his right: stomping, heavy steps through underbrush. A snarl filled the air with the sweet smell of decay.

Finally the old man lifted his eyes and saw what was coming. "Take cover," he told the boy, and Roldin was on his *feet and running before the man had finished saying it. Out of the corner of his eye he saw it coming into the ring of firelight. It was a large, hulking monster, skin covered with scales, horns jutting from its head. It didn't look exactly the same, but somehow Roldin knew this was the creature from the house that had killed that family. Even while his legs carried him away at full speed, anger flashed in his heart and his hand went to his dagger impulsively. He longed to live, but in that moment he longed for that thing to be dead even more. What modicum of revenge could he possibly inflict on that monster?*

He willed his legs to continue his flight. The silent ringing screeched in his ears like the wail of the dead. Roldin expected, at any moment, to hear the old man's dying scream. He was preparing himself to deal with the guilt.

Instead, he heard something very different.

There was an otherworldly howl that filled the forest around him. Roldin stopped running so suddenly that he tripped and fell. He looked back and saw the man standing over his fire, a sword of impossibly black metal in his hands, and the beast impaled on the other end of it.

The creature grabbed at him, but was out of reach. It seemed to grow another arm with a claw on the other end that lashed out, but the man side-stepped it skillfully. He twisted his sword and withdrew it from the creature's body. Black smoke oozed from the wound. The thing seemed to start to recover, and a deep growl came from its throat, but the old man lifted the blade on high and slashed down with all his might, cleaving the beast nearly in two. As it lay writhing on the ground the man studied it in the firelight, seemingly looking for something. Then he lifted the sword and stabbed the creature once, very forcefully, and the beast vanished in a billowing expanse of black smoke that hugged the ground like a fog until it disappeared.

And, just like that, the wailing Dread in Roldin's ears ceased. All that remained of the creature, that he could see, was a small black stone in the dirt in front of the fire, about the size of a man's palm, cloven in half by the dark sword that Varcus held in both hands.

The old man stood up straight, sighed, and bent down to retrieve a cloth from his pack. He cleaned sooty, black ash from his sword with quick, vigorous wipes. Roldin could do nothing but stare. He had no idea what he had just witnessed.

"You're safe, at least for now," Varcus said. The boy crawled to his feet and slowly went back towards the fire.

"It's…is it…?" he asked.

"Only for the time being," the old man answered. "It can be summoned again, but hopefully not anytime soon. We can only hope, eh?" Varcus reached for the two halves of the stone that had fallen where the creature had died. It was dark, just like the smoke, and just like the sword the man carried. He threw one piece to Roldin, who barely caught it. It felt unusually cold in his hands, just like the feeling of their claws on him had been. "Heartstone," the old man said. "Only way to kill one. Only way to summon one. Quite a conundrum, isn't it?"

Roldin stared at it, then at the old man, then at the place where the creature had died. "What…what was it?"

Varcus sat down by his fire, retrieving the scabbard for his blade from where he had hidden it in his bedroll, and sheathed his weapon. "You really don't know, do you?" he asked. He looked at Roldin curiously. "That, my boy, was a demon."

So it was true, he thought. The worst possibility he'd imagined. It made sense, of course. There were many odd things in the world, Roldin knew: creatures at the bottom of the sea, creatures in the sky, creatures in the caves in the deep places that sometimes came out to hunt little children. Demons were real, this much he understood, but no one ever talked about them openly.

"I came here because I'd heard stories of demon attacks in this town for the last several weeks. Something was drawing them here, and I came to find out what – or who – that was."

"I thought you said you were a hunter?"

"I am. I hunt demons." The old man leaned forward and fixed Roldin with a serious gaze; the fire that sat between him and Roldin made the shadows in his eyes deepen. "And these demons are hunting you.*"*

Roldin could feel the color drain from his face. "I don't understand...why? What do they want with me?"

"Your soul," he said.

"How...I don't..."

Varcus shook his head sadly. "Your soul has been marked. Demons want blood, normally. This sustains them when they are summoned here, and gives them power when they go back to whatever hell they come from. But a soul — especially the soul of a child — is infinitely more valuable. Once you're marked, the demon that has a right to it will stop at nothing to get it."

Roldin felt lightheaded, but he was determined not to lose the wonderful dinner he had just eaten, for no other reason than base practicality. He took a steadying breath. "How does something like that happen?"

Varcus stroked his beard. "I take it you didn't give your soul willingly?" Roldin shook his head in response. "Then the only way your soul could be marked would be by a close relative who shares your blood, along with a drop of your own blood. Brother, sister..."

"Father..." Roldin finished.

"You really think your father could do that?"

The boy didn't have to think long. "Yes," he admitted. Then he had a realization. "You said something about a drop of my own blood?"

"Yes, for the strongest link, that's also needed."

Roldin held up his palm to his face — the wound was still not fully healed. The boy closed his eyes, processing all he had been told. After weeks of hard living he couldn't muster strong feelings about it. He just felt numb. "Why would he do it?"

"What kind of man is your father?"

"He...not a good one." The boy looked deep into the fire and lost himself in the swirling flames. The silence lingered.

Varcus took out another flask from his pack and took a deep swig, and then handed it to the boy. It took a moment before he noticed it, and took it gingerly. He drank before he could ask what it was. The strong liquor coursed down his throat like the fire in front of him. It did manage to jar him back to reality, however.

The old man took another drink himself. "It's curious that you've survived this long, if I'm being perfectly honest. Three men were recently found dead...eviscerated, really, in a tavern in Neppeth. That's what drew me here initially."

Roldin sat up. "They're dead?"

Varcus looked surprised. "You saw them? Did you notice the tattoos on their arms?"

The boy nodded. "I also saw one of these," and he held up the heartstone half in his hand.

"The relationship between cultist and demon is a tenuous one. They depend upon people to call them, but they also see people as expendable. Whatever demon you've attracted must be powerful indeed to risk being so callous with its followers." Varcus tugged on his beard so hard that Roldin worried he would pull it out. The old man shook his head as if to clear it, and took a deep breath. His voice was grave. "Boy, I'm sorry to say that there is nothing that can be done. There's no method anyone has ever discovered to un-mark a soul. The demon will come, and will continue to come, until it gets what it feels it is owed."

The boy nodded, finally hearing the truth that he had been living with for weeks. "I've been running this long. At least I'm sort of warned when they come."

"Warned?"

"I call it the Dread. What's the ringing sound I hear when they're near, and this feeling I get in my stomach?"

The old man paused, an appraising look on his face. "Ah, interesting. Well that's a bit of luck right there. As I said, your soul is marked, and not only to the demon who was promised it. A marked soul gives out an indication of sorts when demons are close, an aura, to let them know your soul is available, so to speak. Seems you can hear the same thing they do, which you have been able to use to your advantage. Not sure if it's your youth or something else that lets you do so. Most people whose souls are marked don't live out the day, and don't realize what any of it means until it's too late. But…you seem to have been very resourceful so far, indeed."

Varcus looked at him inquisitively. "You know, demons may be vile creatures, but they have a sense of honor about them. Your soul has been marked, and that will be common knowledge to all of their kind. Weird to say, but you likely don't have much to fear from any demon but the one who has laid claim to you. They won't dare kill you if your soul is marked for another, for their punishment in their realm would be worse than anything we could hope to inflict."

He bent down and picked up his sword and drew it. Roldin leaned back where he sat near the fire. "This sword is made from iron that fell from the sky," he pointed to the night sky above them, "commonly called moon-iron. Legend says that is also where the demons come from, that this is metal from their world, and it can harm them more than our normal steel can. I don't know if the origin is true, but it's like poison to them." He twirled the sword with a flourish, then reversed his grip and presented it before the boy, the blade resting in the crook of his arm.

Roldin took it. Other than the very dark blade, it looked like any other sword. The weight of it sagged in his weak-armed grip. Varcus took his weapon back. "It's also a hard metal, and is more likely to pierce the demon's heartstone without chipping. You can slay a demon without it, but every little bit helps." He shrugged. The old man sheathed his sword and stroked his beard again, studying the boy more. "You need to constantly be on the move, and I always travel anyway. Plus, you have an interesting ability to 'hear' when demons are near. I could make use of that."

The old man seemed to come to a decision, and nodded to himself. "It'll be hard for you to be on your own. You can travel with me. In turn, I can teach you how to defend yourself. How to use sword, bow, dagger, and axe. How to fight demons and how to defeat them. Maybe, you can use what I teach you to fend them off. Maybe it will prolong your life for a few years, though I can't promise anything."

Roldin was too shocked to breathe. He looked up at the man who loomed impossibly large before him. The thought of no longer being alone brought tears to the edge of his eyes. "You think I could survive this way?"

Varcus shrugged. "Who knows? Eventually it will catch up to you. It won't be a good life, sad to say. You will be on the run until the day you die. But if learning to defend yourself gives you a few years, even that is something you could cherish, eh?" He clapped the boy on the shoulder. "So, what do you say?"

The boy was speechless. For the first time in a long time, Roldin dared to let himself hope.

There was not another attack that night. He slept the rest of the night and into midmorning, the first restful sleep he'd had in weeks. Varcus woke him, handed him a share of his baggage, and let him chew on a candy as they left the forest and started down the main road.

Roldin looked back as they walked. He could see Neppeth, its gates looming large and dark, grow smaller. Soon it was completely out of sight, and he allowed himself an audible sigh of relief. The boy was suddenly knocked off balance from a strong slap to the back of his head.

Varcus grunted. "Never let your guard down. Not even if

it seems like everything is perfectly safe...especially then. Let this be your first lesson."

He rubbed the back of his head and fought back a grimace. The boy struggled to stand, dropping his pack as he did so. As he put it back over his shoulders the man lashed out a second time. Roldin saw it coming out of the corner of his eyes and lifted a hand in reflex. The strike still landed, but half the force fell on his arm.

"You learn quickly," the old man said with a curt nod. The two of them continued. The boy was content to face the road ahead of him, happy to leave the town behind, and wondered what was waiting for him over the next hill. Roldin gripped the dagger on his belt with his small hand and promised himself he would be ready for whatever it was.

CHAPTER 10
A FIRE THAT BURNS BRIGHT

Rain was falling in sheets as Roldin made his way through the town, leaning heavily on his crutch. All was quiet. He watched the rain thump against the wood of the plankways and feared again what tomorrow would bring. Was he ready? Was the town?

As if in answer, a disturbance to his left drew his attention. His hand drifted to the axe at his belt, but as his eyes won their fight against the rainy darkness he let it drop. An old man emerged out of the shadows of a house with a large pack on his back, and two young men followed him, likewise burdened with their belongings. The man looked around warily for any patrols, his grey head a dull blur in the torchlight, and he held one hand over his eyes to shield from the rain.

He saw Roldin standing there, and the two simply stared at each other for a moment. Then the man rose up to his full height, defiance etched on his craggy face, and bid his two sons forward. They were big lads, Roldin could tell, though they hunched under the demon slayer's gaze as they went.

"I have to think of my family," the old man said, his eyes hard, his fists clenched. "We're all going to die tomorrow and most of these people are too foolish to see it. You can stop me, but please, let them go."

Roldin watched as the two men—just boys, really—took off through the plankways and ran towards the forest. "They could have been a good help tomorrow, they look strong," he said. "But I understand. I won't stop you."

The old man hesitated. He looked Roldin up and down, though he couldn't have seen much in the darkness. "I've heard stories of you, Benirus. Some call you a thief, a liar, a backstabber...a coward, on the run your whole life."

"Adren, most likely," Roldin said with a shrug. "They say many things about me. Some of that is even true, I guess. But a coward?" He turned his face up to the falling rain and let it wash over him with a smile. "Definitely."

The elder frowned over at him. "Then why in the name of all the Sacreds don't you run too, then?"

"Because," Roldin said slowly, "it's time I do more than just survive." He nodded towards the direction the boys had gone. "Do what you think is best for your family. It's what a good father should do."

The old man nodded, started to say something else, then took off. Roldin didn't watch him go, but he hoped that they could make it out of town without running into any patrols. He felt that no man should be faulted by his peers for doing what he thought best, and Roldin wished to spare the three that much. This made him look around, and it struck him that the plankways were emptier than they should have been. Just as Roldin was wondering where the civilian guards that should have been on patrol were, something hit him from behind.

The demon slayer was propelled forward, hard, and slammed into the plankways. Two sets of hands held him down as another reached for his axe. Roldin pushed up against the hands but they were quite strong. He turned his head just enough to recognize one of the giant miners that he had met earlier. "What are you doing?" he struggled to say. They didn't respond.

He suddenly stopped resisting, letting himself fall completely to the deck. This tipped one of the miners over and Roldin reached behind himself for the man's tunic, grabbed, and pulled him forward with a jerk. The unbalanced miner fell with a yell through the railings and into the floodwaters below. A second punched Roldin hard in the side of the head, but Roldin was no longer pinned down. He caught the next punch with his palm as the third miner got Roldin's dark-bladed axe free and backed away.

Roldin kicked with his good leg and knocked the second miner back, though not far. The one with his axe continued to back away, an uncertain look on his face. Roldin got to his feet just as the second miner renewed his attack. The big man lunged, throwing punches left and right. The demon slayer dodged them easily, even while limping, and found an opening. As the big man thrust at his head, Roldin ducked and punched hard into the man's upper thigh, then he launched a second fist into his stomach. The miner fell over, the breath knocked out of him.

The demon slayer bent to pick up his crutch and approached the third, who still had Roldin's axe in his hands, his eyes wide. "W-we're supposed to b-bring you," he stammered.

"Where?" Roldin growled.

"The tavern, to…"

Roldin didn't bother to hear more. He lunged forward and grabbed his axe, knocking the miner aside and rushing through the town as fast as he could shuffle in the blinding rain. He threw his crutch away, barely dodging the various traps and holes that had been planted throughout the plankways.

The tavern's inner lamps were lit. He rounded the last corner and crashed through the door.

Wull was at the end of the bar, his hands tied and a gag over his mouth. Another miner standing behind him froze as the demon slayer entered. Roldin saw Penny near the fireplace, hands bound in front of her, her hair held in a tight grip by an old man he'd seen in the town several times.

"Silas, you don't have to do this," Penny said.

The old man, a miner in his younger years and still strong in his old age, pulled harder to silence her and held a crude knife to her throat. "So you're here alone," he said to the demon slayer. "Guess those fools didn't do as I wanted."

Roldin held his hands up as Silas pulled on Penny's hair again, causing a small scream to escape the barmaid's throat. "What do you want?" Roldin asked. "Coin? I have plenty. I can give you as much as you want."

"Oh, I have more coin than I could ever spend," the old man chortled. "It's not what you can do for me. It's what you can do for Yunirax. Time is running out and my demon lord is worried that you will make the wrong choice on the deal."

Roldin hid his surprise and shook his head. "It was never a choice," he said. "If Yunirax wants a soul it'll have to pry it from my body in the morning."

"Yunirax would much rather have your son's," he sneered. Penny gasped. The old man laughed at her. "Oh yes, I know your secret, girl. Once I overheard the two of you the first night and discovered that you knew the demon slayer I figured who fathered the little bastard of yours! It all fit into place. Once I told Yunirax," Silas closed his eyes and smiled. "Oh, the riches I was offered for my service." He looked again at Roldin and smiled a mirthless, gap-toothed grin. "So here's the new deal, demon slayer. You go now, mark his soul for my lord Yunirax, and we'll all walk out of this alive. Do not, and I'll start the destruction of this town early with pretty Penny, here."

The miner who stood behind Wull shifted uncomfortably. "This isn't what we discussed, Silas," he said uncertainly. "You said we were going to make it so no one got hurt tomorrow."

"And so we are," Silas seethed. "No more than necessary." The old man reached over and smelled the woman's hair with a smile. "Shouldn't have dismissed me all those times so quickly, little Penny. I always told you you'd regret it."

Roldin hefted his axe in his hands. "This is not a deal you can make. Whatever Yunirax promised you—"

"More coin than you can fathom, and it is already in my possession," Silas said. Roldin saw Penny move her hands. They were out of Silas' sight, and the old man didn't see her grab Roldin's dagger, which had been hidden in the folds of her skirts. "You have no chips with which to bargain with me, brute. Either the boy's soul dies tonight, or hers." He held the knife tighter against her neck. Penny's hands only faltered slightly at the pain; her fingers found their way around the dagger and pulled, slowly.

"You're making a mistake, Silas," Roldin said. "Consorting with demons always is. This is not going to end well for you."

"Oh really?" the old man sneered.

"Really," Penny strained to say. She pulled the

dagger out and, with both hands bound, brought it up and lashed out behind herself blindly. The blade found the old man's cheek and dug deep. He cried in pain but held on to her hair, though the knife fell from his other hand as he brought that one up to his face protectively. She twisted in his grip and turned. A lock of her hair came off in Silas' iron grip. Penny brought the dagger up hard into Silas' chest.

The miner guarding Wull started forward towards them but Roldin threw his dark-bladed axe. It founds its mark in the post right next to the miner's head. The big man looked at the axe handle that was inches from his face, saw the unarmed but still dangerous demon slayer in front of him, and thought better of taking any action. He held up his hands in submission.

Penny left the dagger in Silas' chest and backed away, staring at the dying man. He sputtered in disbelief as his life left him. Her hands shook. Roldin was at her side in three large steps and put a hand on her shoulder, gently. She jumped anyway, backed away, and regarded the demon slayer coldly. "What was he talking about?" she shrieked. "What deal?"

Roldin tried to calm her, but Penny was having none of it. "The demon came to me last night. That's how I knew they're coming tomorrow. They want me to give them Linder's soul like my father gave mine."

"And you —"

"Never," he said.

"Why didn't you tell me!?" she cried hysterically.

"Because it's not going to happen," Roldin said. "I'm not going to do it. Yunirax cannot touch his soul unless one of us gives it, and I won't let the demon come into this town tomorrow to touch his body, either!"

Penny held his gaze for another moment, then fell into his arms, shaking and crying. Roldin held her and tried to comfort her. He looked over her hair at Wull, who was rubbing his chafed wrists. "Get Jodas," Roldin told him quietly.

The constable gathered the four miners who Silas had recruited. "He told us that we had no way of winning tomorrow, and that the only way was to give the slayer up," the one who Roldin had sent to take a swim in the floodwaters explained to Jodas. He had a blanket wrapped around him and was shivering. "He didn't say anything about hurting Penny or her son. And he definitely didn't say anything about a demon."

"And he paid you too, right?" Roldin asked.

The miners all nodded. One took out a money pouch. "I...I don't want it," he said and threw it at the demon slayer, who caught it and opened it, taking out a coin. Roldin hefted it and squeezed it between his fingers, and threw it to Jodas.

The constable caught it and looked at it oddly. "It feels...too light? And really cold."

"Demon conjured," Roldin said.

The remaining three miners all took their bags of coins from their belts and threw them away from themselves. "Unclean!" one spat.

"So it wasn't even real?" another asked.

"Oh, it's real," Roldin said. "It's gold as much as a real coin is, on a basic level. But when a demon conjures coins — or anything, really — the result is only as good as its understanding of what it's trying to create. It usually comes out as a rather poor attempt at forgery. And it's limited by the demon's own power. It takes something out of them. Whatever demon conjured all these," he said, gesturing to the pouches on the floor, "no doubt is taking a while to recover." He squeezed the coin and it collapsed a little between his fingers. "But, they also apparently don't know that coins aren't hollow."

Jodas looked at all the coin on the floor. "That's quite a fortune down there, though."

The demon slayer shrugged. "If you found a foolish merchant who didn't know how to recognize conjured coins you could maybe make use of it."

"We'll take these coins," the constable said to the miners. "And let's just write this off as the actions of a few desperate fools in a time of crisis."

Roldin eyed them. "We can win tomorrow, no matter what lies Silas was spreading," he said. "Are you still with me?"

All four nodded their heads, and when Jodas excused them they left quickly.

Penny walked up behind Roldin, still shaken. "Wull and I are done," she said, fidgeting with a now shorter bit of hair that hung awkwardly on the side of her head. "I was thinking of heading home."

"Go," he said. "Be with Linder, get some sleep. I'll see you in the morning."

She smiled at him, but it didn't reflect in her eyes. Penny stepped into the rain at a brisk pace. Jodas put a hand on his shoulder. "She's still in shock a little. We see it all the time. I don't think she blames you."

Roldin shook his head. "She probably should. She certainly has the right to."

Jodas said, "I think you need a drink. I sure as hell know I won't be getting any sleep tonight."

The demon slayer laughed. "You and me both. Why

not?"

Roldin took a seat while Jodas stepped behind the bar. "Wull won't mind," he said with a grin and took out a couple of glasses and the last bottle of whiskey that was tucked away behind the bar. "I'm the one who throws all the drunks out and gets the others to pay their tab. I know where they hide the good stuff."

The door opened and Mayor Kinnley came in with a frown on his face. "Heard about Silas, the old fool." He sat down next to Roldin and nodded as Jodas took out a third glass with a questioning glance. Kinnley grinned at the demon slayer and said, "I guess we'll have that drink now."

"No time like the present," Roldin replied with a tight smile. "The threat of certain battle, wounds that aren't yet healed, and the glare of a woman who thinks she hates you — never has a more fitting call for drink been made."

Jodas poured and the three men clinked their glasses in salute before they took their first drink. The constable came around the bar to take a seat on a stool and started rubbing his feet. He finally saw the sword at the mayor's hip. "Well, that's an antique," he said with a laugh. "When was the last time you wore that?"

"When we gallivanted around the legion like young fools," he said. "I haven't even picked it up since. Thought that now was as good a time as any."

"Do you think you still know how to use it?"

"I'm not really sure I ever did. I wasn't exactly a war hero." Kinnley touched the grip of the steel sword sheathed at his side.

Jodas laughed. "You had your share of brave moments. You were a hell of a soldier, that's for sure." The constable leaned over and poured each of them another round. He raised his glass to his old friend. "It would be an honor to fight by your side again."

They downed their whiskey and slammed the glasses down as a peal of thunder worked its way through the tavern's foundations. "Damn the spring," Kinnley said into his glass. "Rain, thunderstorms, and more rain. If this happened any other time of the year we wouldn't be stuck here, and we could make a run for it fast enough to get to safety...."

"We can only run so far, and for so long," Roldin said, staring off into the shadowy corners of the room. "Eventually they catch up. Always do." The men said nothing. Jodas went ahead and poured another round.

Dawn came sooner than any of them would have believed. The three men had abandoned drink in the middle of the night and sobered up on water, bread, and tales. As the sun tried its best to force its way through the storm clouds they left the tavern and watched the town slowly wake. Every face was determined. There was a charge in the air, a well-controlled panic.

"Roldin!" the demon slayer heard, and saw Alys running to him, a drawn look on her face. "Roldin, come with me, quickly!" Jodas and Kinnley nodded for him to go and they continued their walkthrough of the defenses.

"What's wrong?" he asked as he started to hobble as fast as he could beside her.

"Just come," she said, not meeting his eyes.

They arrived at the abandoned house she had been staying in, though even before they reached it Roldin felt the familiar stirring in his gut, and he readied his axe. He rounded the corner to her bedroom and saw a bit of blood on the ground, and then Saeralyx sitting there, cross-legged. The demon looked up at Roldin tranquilly.

The demon slayer shook his head and rounded on Alys, "I told you not to summon—"

"This is my doing," the demon said in its slow, peaceful way. "I called her to summon me. And I'm afraid I was too insistent for her to ignore."

Alys shrugged. "You were pretty loud inside my head. More than the voices normally are."

Saeralyx smiled at her. Roldin put a reassuring hand on Alys' arm and then turned to the demon. "I didn't want you here, my friend," the demon slayer said. "I don't know what those demons will do to you back in your realm if they saw you helping me, or even knew you were here right now. I didn't want to risk you."

"I am beyond their touch now," the demon said quietly, peacefully.

Roldin paused and looked again at his friend. He noticed the demon was vaguely translucent, as if it was having trouble keeping its form. "What's wrong, Saeralyx? What...did you do?"

The demon sighed, deeply. "I have been fascinated by humans for so, so long. I loved your art, I listened to your music, I read your poetry, but I never understood you. I never understood your capacity for beauty, and I wished to. I never understood how your people create so much and are so happy when your lives are so very brief. How you could be in so much pain but not give up." Saeralyx seemed to waver for a moment, then correct itself and shake its head. "Do you remember when we first met?"

Roldin sat down across from the demon, confused. "We...we met when I was fourteen. I'd been running for a few days and fell asleep in the woods. You found me under a log and when I woke, you had caught me dinner and made a fire, and you were sitting there calmly reading a book."

"And what did you do when you saw me?"

Roldin laughed. "I took out my sword and tried to attack you. That's what Varcus taught me demon slayers do."

"And when you attacked me, Roldin Benirus, why do you think I did not fight back?"

The demon slayer paused in thought. "I don't know. I remember I wore myself out swinging at you, and I couldn't even touch you, then I gave up and sat down. Then you watched as I ate the food you made and we talked until dawn, when your summoning was up and you vanished in front of me."

"I never got to finish my book that day."

"That's why I kept it and let you have it the next time I saw you."

"Ah yes, I remember." The demon laughed. "I didn't fight you, Roldin, because I saw something in you that I'd never seen in a human before. You were strong, yet weak. You were wizened and tired, yet young. You were a fighter, but I had watched you before you fell asleep and I had seen you stop and rescue a bird that had fallen out of its nest, even as you ran for your life. You were missing part of yourself, but you also had a warmer soul than many people have with their whole ones."

Roldin shook his head. "No."

"Yes. It radiated from you like a star. I wished to study you. I wanted to see what kind of man you would become, if you lived that long. You were a curiosity." It lifted a pale white hand to one of Roldin's own and squeezed softly, though there was barely any strength in its touch. "And then, you were my friend."

The man returned the gesture, then shook his head. "Saeralyx, why are you here?" he asked.

"Why are you?" it asked in return. "You should be running—you could make it far enough away by yourself that they lose your trail, even with your injuries—but you stay and face the clear likelihood of death, unafraid." The demon closed its eyes; its voice was pained. "I am shamed for the life I led, for the pain and death I have caused your people. We saw them as lesser beings but you have helped me see them as innocents, whose souls sing with beauty that is all too brief. I cannot make up for the lives I took, and especially for the evils of the rest of my kind. But I can try to help you stop them. I, too, can face death with my head held high, as you are."

Roldin opened his mouth to speak but Saeralyx put a hand up to silence him. When it spoke its three voices sounded hollow, as if they were coming from far away. "I finally understand it now. I understand why it is so much better to be a fire that burns bright before it fades away, than an ember that smolders forever." Saeralyx seemed to falter for a moment, and Roldin reached out and grabbed the demon and supported it gently.

Saeralyx continued quietly, "Our conjuration power is limited, but only by what we give of ourselves with it. If a demon would give all that it had to give, it could accomplish wonders never before seen by my kind or mankind, as selflessness is not one of our virtues." The demon reached behind itself and took something off the ground. It was white, about two feet long, and it looked like polished, milky glass. The demon ran its hands over the surface. "I have begun this, but I have yet to finish it. I wanted to say goodbye, first."

"Goodbye? But I don't understand, demons can't—"

Saeralyx shook its head. "We *can* die. It happens when we give too much of ourselves, either here or in our realm, so it is not something that can be taken from us like it can be for you. Our lives only end by our own choosing."

"Don't do this," Roldin pleaded, touching Saeralyx's hands, its face. "There are other ways you could atone if that's what you want. We'll find a way. You've already given me so much."

"I have given you nothing but my conversation and my compassion. But you—you have given me a comprehension of the power of the soul, a power each demon craves, yet none of them understand." The demon sighed, its three voices singing in harmony. "You asked me once, long ago, why this was done to you. Why an evil person, more deserving, wasn't given your fate. Over time that changed; as you grew older you believed that you deserved what life had given you, though I think the question lingered in your heart underneath all of your sorrow, crying out like a confused child. I didn't have an answer for you then, but I think I finally understand now." Saeralyx touched Roldin in the center of his forehead with a lightly feathered finger. The man closed his eyes at the gentle touch.

"You have done nothing to deserve your fate. It is, instead, because of your own goodness and innocence that this was done to you. It was all you had left and you transformed it into your greatest strength. Don't you see? It has kept so many from harm that could have wallowed in suffering. This has happened to you because it could happen to no one else. You were the right person, in the right place, at the right time, and for that, sweet, dear boy, I am so very sorry."

The demon slayer's shoulders slumped. Saeralyx drew the man into an embrace and held him there for a time. Then it pushed him away gently. The demon lifted the object into its lap and cradled it. "Now, let me give back to you. It will be the instrument of your freedom. I will help you on your search for peace, Roldin Benirus.

May you find it before your life ends."

Saeralyx moved its hands over the object and it slowly changed shape, accompanied by a blinding light. As that light grew more brilliant, the demon began to fade.

"Saeralyx, don't," Roldin pleaded. He reached for his friend but the demon was already too ethereal to be touched. "Don't leave me...."

"I will never leave you, now," the demon said with the last of its breath.

As the light faded Saeralyx was nowhere to be seen. There was no heartstone left behind. All that sat on the floor was an axe, very much like Roldin's, but pure white instead of dark. It gleamed in the meager light of the cloudy dawn; the surpassingly beautiful and smooth curves of its shaft, which looked like opaque burnished glass, was in sharp contrast with the razor edge of its blade. It was a weapon, that much was clear, but it was also the most heart-wrenching work of art Roldin had ever seen.

The demon slayer picked it up. It was unnaturally warm to the touch.

Alys wept quietly behind him.

CHAPTER 11

JUST LIKE IN THE STORY

Roldin sat quietly at the end of the town, under the towering spires of Mount Everdare, and near the flooded mine entrance. He let the rain wash over him. The man rubbed his hands, working feeling back into them. The bleeding spot on his palm still oozed slightly and he picked at it like he always did.

The gleaming axe was on his lap. Roldin hefted it; there was a presence to it, a weight that would crush bone and shear limbs, but it was also light. It would be a swift weapon, indeed. He'd never held anything like it, yet at that moment he wasn't sure if he could bring himself to use it at all.

Penny put a hand on his shoulder. Roldin stirred. He cleared his throat and wiped his eyes quickly as he stood, though it was a meaningless gesture as the rain fell steadily around him. "How are you holding up?" he asked.

"I'm fine," she said. "Alys told me what happened with Saeralyx. I'm so sorry, Roldin."

The demon slayer slumped and shook his head. "I still don't understand. We've been friends for a long time, but I don't deserve something like this." He held up the axe and studied it as it shone bright, even in the hidden morning light. "Saeralyx never did anything without reason, without purpose. This isn't just a weapon, but…I don't know its true purpose, or how this will set me free like I was told. But no matter what this axe does it's not worth its…" He growled in frustration. "No, I know Saeralyx was a demon, but it was a she, not just…not just a thing! She was my friend, the closest thing to a mother I ever had, and it wasn't worth her life!"

Roldin turned and threw the axe. It spun through the rain and imbedded itself in the stone near the entrance to the mine. The demon slayer stared at it—any other axe would chip and break at such a throw. "Saeralyx was right about you, I think," Penny said to his back. "It's why you stayed. It's why you didn't take the way out, and why you…why you didn't give them Linder. You are a good person, despite everything that's happened to you." She squeezed his arm and fought to meet his eyes. "No matter what happens today, no matter if they kill you or they take your soul, the demons can never take that away from you. That's worth sacrificing something for."

The demon slayer said nothing for a time. He took the axe by its pearl-like shaft and freed it from the rock wall as easily as if he had drawn it from water. Roldin felt the oddly warm presence of the axe in his hand, then placed it in the loop in his belt. "I will wield this, but not for me. I want you to be able to tell our son that a demon named Saeralyx gave her life to protect him today. I want to give my friend that honor." Penny nodded her head, and enveloped Roldin in a gentle hug.

#

Mayor Kinnley stepped out onto his porch into the rain-soaked morning. He had on some armor—a patch-worked cuirass of steel and leather from his youth. It barely fit him now. On his side he wore his legion sword that had obviously seen better days. He let out a breath. He could see out over the town; saw his townspeople gathered against what was coming, and he was proud.

Some turned and gasped when they saw him. Jodas joined him at the bottom of the walkway from his house, his spear in his hand. "I can see you suited up," the constable said.

"I wasn't up all night drinking for nothing," Kinnley said with an easy drawl. "I suppose it's almost time. Where's the slayer?"

"I'm here," Roldin said. The demon slayer was wearing his splint and mail armor. A simple leather helmet adorned his head. He still leaned heavily on his crutch. Penny was next to him and gave the mayor a nod. Alys followed not far behind, a bounce in her step and a smile on her face. The mayor shook his head at the odd woman.

Kinnley gripped Roldin's hand in greeting. "Soft morning for a battle," he said.

The demon slayer laughed. "It may work in our favor. If we get the demons up in the air the rain may help hide our movements on the ground."

"We could use the Sacreds' help today in any way we can," the mayor said, eyeing the sky briefly.

"Whatever makes you sleep better," Roldin said. "Personally, I just want to be able to kill them before they kill us."

Penny, Alys, the constable and the mayor stood on top of a house in the middle of the town to get the best vantage point, and Roldin joined them once he finished slowly climbing the makeshift stairs. From there they could see the townspeople at their marks. Kinnley shouted some more orders, adjusting them here or there. The demon slayer nodded his approval.

The rain came down harder, battering the already scared villagers. Dawn came and went, though it was hard to tell through the clouds and rain. As an hour crept by with no demonic sign, some of the townspeople became restless. Alys started wringing her hair out. Penny began tittering nervously.

Roldin was still as a statue, and kept looking out into the trees that dotted the flooded landscape. He put a hand to his stomach absently. "They're here," he said. Penny and Alys thought they could see figures in the mist. They were indistinguishable at first, just darker shadows in the already grey expanse. Then they materialized into shapes. A few of the townspeople yelled an alert. All eyes went to the flooded road.

They were men, eight of them, each one covered in robes, water-logged and shivering. They leaned heavily on staffs or paused against trees as they made their advance. The citizens of Road's End stared on in confusion. No one was sure what to make of it.

Then, from behind the men, eight more shapes came into view. They were of varying sizes; some were hulking and misshapen, others were smaller. All were horrifying.

"Eight," Roldin said, letting out a long breath.

Alys suddenly clapped and gasped in delight. "An army! Just like in the story!" she observed with giddiness.

The townspeople watched as each demon drew itself up, making itself larger, and let out an otherworldly howl that came from the bowels of hell. Each citizen stepped back involuntarily. Some prayed to the Sacreds. One leaned over a railing and was noisily sick.

The eight men walking in front of the demons

stopped. Each took off their robes and let them drift off into the waters. They were naked underneath. Their chests, arms, and legs were all covered with cut marks oozing with fresh blood. As one they lifted their heads up and faced the falling rain, exposing their necks. Each demon turned to one of the cultists and lashed out quickly, lacerating their throats with a single swipe. The demons enveloped them, the grisly details of their ritual luckily blocked from the view of most. Even so, the witnesses screamed at the brutality.

The cultist's sacrifice made each demon seem to grow, in size and in presence. The demon army let out another primal scream that echoed off of Mount Everdare and was swallowed by the rain.

Roldin gripped his crutch hard. As if in no particular hurry, he worked his way down the stairs and began to limp over to the edge of the town's palisade.

"Eight?" Jodas asked as the demon slayer advanced. "Can...can you kill eight?" he called out to Roldin.

The demon slayer grimaced. "Haven't before, but today seems a good day to try."

"How about a speech, Roldin?" the mayor asked a little nervously. "We could use some inspiration right now."

"What?" Roldin asked. "Speech? We don't have time for a speech," he said, pointing at the eight demons that lingered beyond their makeshift palisade. "We have to go kill them."

Alys jumped up and down and waved her hand. "Mayor! Mayor, let me!" she said. All eyes turned to her, and the small woman paused and smiled awkwardly. "I...I just wanted to say good luck, to all of us! Things look bad, but it'll be fine. Because we have Roldin!" She gestured to the demon slayer, who stood hunched over his crutch and had a bruise forming under his eye from the fight he'd had overnight with the miners. Of all the heroes described in all the stories, he certainly was not looking the part at that moment.

Alys went on, undeterred. "He'll do this! Roldin will, I promise! He's strong and tough. Oh, oh, and he has a Saeral-axe!" She froze her mouth open in a manic grin.

Penny turned, her eyes wide, her mouth agape. Roldin stared at her with an unreadable expression. The townspeople looked on, confused.

"Ooooh," she said, turning red. "That was a bit insensitive, wasn't it?"

After a beat, Roldin laughed loud, and hard.

Penny was still stunned but Alys joined in, and Roldin made his way over to her. He put his hands on her shoulders, smiled sweetly after he finished laughing, looked her in the eye, and said, "Don't *ever* say that again."

"Right," she said. "Insensitive. Understood!"

"Roldin," a voice called from the flooded road. "Your time is up." The townspeople stirred. No one could quite place what the voice sounded like, but all would say the tone was almost female. One of the demons came closer to the town, alone. It floated above the water on wings of red flesh and bone. The body looked wet, almost like lizard skin, and the shape was also a vague idea of what a woman would look like if it was drawn from distant memory tinged with a nightmare. Its face was a pantomime of a woman's as well, full of hard edges and jagged lines.

"I'm here, Yunirax," Roldin said as he hobbled forward to the edge of a plankway and close to their palisade barrier. "If you haven't guessed, the answer is no."

"I'm sad to hear it," the demon said. "I must say, I'm surprised you're still here. This is not like you, boy."

Roldin stood, his dark axe in one hand and his crutch gripped in the other. "This is true," he admitted. "I've been running a long, long time." He let his crutch fall to the plankway. It landed with a dull thud against the wood. The demon slayer put all of his weight on his left leg. He grimaced at the pain that shot through his thigh and into his entire body, but it held. "But right now, I'm tired of running."

Yunirax shook its head and turned to the other seven demons behind it. "Bring me his soul. Kill the rest."

They complied.

Seven demons charged the town. Two of them took flight and came faster than the rest. They both had maws with rows of teeth, claws of razors on their hands, and were carried into the sky by black wings. They flew over the palisade and dove at Roldin with their fangs bared.

He stood his ground. The demon slayer waited until the very last moment, when one of the demons was almost upon him. He switched his axe to his left hand. With his right, he withdrew the white gleaming axe that was hidden behind him under his cloak and brought it around with a scream of defiance. The demon that flew at him took the strike clear in its reptilian-like torso. The otherworldly blade cut the demon in half. With his left arm Roldin brought the dark moon-iron axe up from below and into the ruins of its chest before the body had a chance to fall to the ground. There was an audible crack, and the demon vanished in two separate hazes of smoke.

The second descended. Roldin ducked under one swipe of a talon, then brought the white axe around and sheared off an arm. His other axe crushed a knee. The demon fell, writing in pain. Roldin raised both axes above his head and brought each down once, twice, three times in twin strikes. Scales and protective skin shattered, and another crack was heard as the demon vanished. Two pieces of heartstone lazily rolled around the plankways and fell through cracks, falling into the flood waters below. Roldin looked down with wonder at the gleaming axe, made by — of –the only demon who ever had a soul.

The five other demons that descended upon the town of Road's End saw the fate of their kin. They paused.

A cheer went up from the townspeople. Roldin Benirus stood tall, dark and light axes in his hands, and stared defiantly at the demons before him.

"I said bring me his soul!" Yunirax screamed behind them. Whatever dread they had of the demon slayer was outmatched by the wrath of their leader. The five continued their charge. Each had to form wings to fly over the wooden palisade that came between them and the town.

"Now!" Roldin screamed, and the demon slayer turned and disappeared into the house nearest him. A dozen townspeople suddenly popped up from behind wooden doors in ruined houses and launched spears, pots, pans, chunks of iron — anything they had — at the demons. The five were forced to halt their advance to block and dodge the assault.

That gave Roldin time to get to another set of walkways, only slightly slowed by his leg. "Over here!" he bellowed. The five demons descended, flying through the barrage of projectiles that peppered them. The demon slayer dove into a house and kept going. One of the demons snarled and changed shape from a flying lizard to something more akin to an armadillo. It formed up into a heavily scaled ball and rolled forward, destroying the house, turning it to kindling, but not finding Roldin within. It unfurled and looked around in fury to see the man running down an opposite walkway. It charged after him.

A second demon caught up to Roldin on the plankway and descended with a screech. It lashed out with a claw. He blocked with one axe, then brought his other gleaming axe around and bit into its side. The demon howled in pain, but still advanced. Roldin ran, the demon hot on his heels.

The three other demons still flew above the town. One went to dive for Roldin but the man escaped into the cover of a house, quickly pursued by another. It landed on the roof, its wings changing into large clawed feet that climbed and jumped from house to house to catch up to him. As it did it landed on a rooftop that instantly collapsed. The demon fell through and landed on a bed of sharpened wooden stakes. It howled in pain, then struggled to change its shape to escape.

Kinnley emerged from the shadows in the darkened house, sword in hand, and began hacking at it. Jodas yelled a charge and came at it from another side, spear at the ready, stabbing the demon repeatedly. Between the wooden stakes and the weapons it was a blur of scales and fur and anything it could struggle to conjure to block the incoming attacks. As it writhed, trapped, Jodas' spear jammed down into its middle. Kinnley joined with his own blade, rending scales and flesh easily as its forms shifted in panic. One of the attacks found its heartstone and the demon vanished in smoke. The two men looked at each other, and after a moment of stunned disbelief, screamed in triumph.

#

Roldin ran through a series of hollowed-out houses and covered alleyways, their roofs giving him protection from above. One demon was still chasing him and was slowly advancing, crashing through doorframes and wooden walls as it came. The demon slayer ran through an open doorway, turned, and seemed to be waiting for his fate. As the demon leapt through the air to reach him Roldin quickly closed the iron jail cell door in its face. The demon hit it with a loud thud and was dazed. The demon slayer smiled and brought one axe down on its head, and the other up from below, trapping its body between the two weapons.

On cue, four miners emerged from other rooms in the house armed with pickaxes and they wailed on the trapped demon, striking its back as if it were a hunk of rock in their own mine. Eventually one of the picks struck true and found the heartstone and the demon vanished. Roldin nodded his thanks and kept going.

#

Two demons flew overhead trying to find the slayer in the maze of wooden houses. A few townspeople continued their barrage of whatever they could find that could be thrown. One demon, angered by a spear that lodged in its leg, screamed and dove for one of the villagers. The man ducked into the house, and as the demon landed and reached in with a clawed hand and a snarl it heard a hollow voice in its own demonic language yell, "Benirus is behind you!" Confused by the sudden ally, it turned, then dove into a set of houses. It found itself in a maze of wooden alleyways and hollowed out houses. "Left!" the voice yelled, and the demon obeyed. "Right!" it guided, and the demon turned. "Ahead! Keep going!" was the next prompt, and the demon roared and charged ahead, seeing an empty space ahead of it.

It emerged from the warren of wooden shacks and into the rain, looking for its prey. The deck it was running on collapsed and the demon fell into a cage. A door closed on top of it. Just as it was going to turn to mist to slip through, the demon heard a click and a grinding noise and the entire cage fell into the water. The demon was stuck fast. It clawed in panic, gasping for breath, trying to force through the strong bars that held it, but they were reinforced and the demon was unable to will sufficient strength to break them.

Alys emerged from one of the houses, a curved cone of thin sheet-iron in her hands, and put it back to her lips. "Idiot!" she yelled hollowly into it in demonic, then jumped up and down in a cheer.

#

The demon that was a rolling ball of bone and scales continued its pursuit. It destroyed anything it came into contact with, splintering sharpened wooden stakes and houses alike. It saw the demon slayer again, running towards the tavern, and it continued its deadly roll. As it neared the tavern, Penny, Wull, and a dozen other townspeople emerged from windows, from hidden passages underneath the plankways, and from covered nooks above and pelted the demon with bottles. Each broke upon its skin, and the demon laughed at the petty display as it barreled forward.

Penny then ran from her hiding place with a lit torch and threw it to Roldin as he ran past her. The demon barreled near the tavern just as Roldin turned and dropped the torch to the plankways that lay sheltered from the rain by the porch of the Goldenpick tavern. A trail of whiskey went up in flames and snaked its way to the approaching monster, and exploded when it met the soaked demon. The alcohol-infused fire ate through the demon's scaly hide. It unfurled with a crash and contorted in agony.

"Now!" Roldin called. Five more miners emerged from the tavern with pickaxes in hand and landed blows onto the howling demon.

The final flying demon landed nearly on top of Roldin. It lashed out with a whip-like hand, barbed with razors, and managed to wrap around his arm. It tugged, and his dark axe went flying down the plankways. The whip cut deep through mail and into his left arm. The demon slayer ducked under a slash of the demon's other scythe-tipped arm, but then a tail came around and tripped him. Roldin fell to the ground but lashed out with his gleaming axe, slicing off a foot, forcing the demon back.

The large demon behind him was finally destroyed by the fire and the pickaxes, which had found its heartstone, and the demon armed with the whip growled deep within its throat. It backed away and began to change its form, growing slowly larger, and dove off into the flood waters. The townspeople looked for it but it had vanished in the murky deep below.

It was then that Yunirax joined the fight, descending out of the air with a screech like a bird of prey. It landed on top of the tavern and buffeted with its wings. A few of the townspeople who were positioned there went flying off and landed in the flood waters or on the decks below.

Roldin screamed a challenge, but it was cut off by a rumbling sound behind him. The demon slayer turned just as the demon rose from the waters, with a dozen tentacles jutting out of a squid-like body, like a sea monster from an old sailor's tale. One of the tentacles lunged at him. He dove, but was knocked aside bodily by another and hit a wall with a crash. The demon reared up, tentacles snaking forward, but it was interrupted by a mining cart filled with stones that crashed into the outstretched limbs from the side, crushing them. Kinnley and Jodas were behind it. "Go get her!" Kinnley called as they regrouped with six of the miners, and surrounded the demon from the plankways.

The demon slayer climbed one of their makeshift ladders set up in an alleyway and emerged on top of the tavern roof. "I'm here, Yunirax!" he yelled to his rival.

The demon turned, sneering. The feminine face was contorted in rage. It began to grow larger. Its wings vanished and its hands shifted, and two barbed swords appeared out of nowhere and grafted themselves to its claws. Roldin twirled his white axe in his hand. "I don't know where you got that pretty thing," Yunirax hissed, "but I'll make sure to bury you with it!"

With a cry the two crashed into one another. The demon stood nearly five feet taller than Roldin, with arms longer than his body, but he was faster. He dove under strikes, evaded kicks, and parried swords like a madman. It was all he could do to keep the demon at bay.

#

"Lead it towards the mine entrance!" Kinnley screamed behind him. The miners, now joined by other townspeople who stood on decks on either side of the flooded street, pelted the squid-demon with anything they had, running towards the mountain as they did so, leading the creature on. Alys joined them, a home-made slingshot in her hands, and took careful aim. She waited until the demon advanced onto one side of the flooded street and lashed out with its tentacles, preparing to render one of the miners apart, and let loose. The vial flew through the air and landed on the demon's back with a crash, and burst. Moon-iron laced water met the demon's skin with a hiss.

The squid-like demon howled and turned, and Alys made sure to wave before she kept running towards the mine with the others. The demon advanced in hot, angry pursuit.

#

Roldin parried and ducked under strikes, his gleaming white axe a blur in the pouring rain, as the bitter enemies hurled blow after blow at one another. He landed a mighty hack on Yunirax's left arm and a barbed sword dropped from its mangled hand, vanishing in a swirl of smoke and black ash. The demon slayer turned and leapt to the next building over, landing in a roll, and faced his attacker with a roar of challenge. Yunirax followed with a screech, changing to a series of snake-like tendrils of mists that slithered through the air. Roldin leapt back as they swirled around his legs and Yunirax reformed in front of him, its left hand grown anew.

The demon managed a strong kick on Roldin's bleeding left arm. He faltered in pain, before screaming, bringing his axe around to bury it in Yunirax's side. The demon gripped onto the axe with a taloned hand and struggled with the demon slayer, slowing pulling the blade out of its side and lunging at his exposed neck with its teeth. Roldin jerked back and evaded the maw, then returned with a head butt in Yunirax's face. Both demon and demon slayer reeled and backed away from one another.

#

The townspeople, led by Kinnley, ran for the mines. The squid-demon was faster and swam forward in the flood waters, rising up before them in challenge with its tentacles outstretched and a screech leaving its mouth. Alys aimed another vial at it, striking it in the face, and it recoiled, backing away further.

Kinnley, Jodas, and several of the miners advanced on it, weapons drawn, and hacked at it to make it hasten its retreat. The demon recovered and lashed out, grew barbs on its tentacles, and struck out at the men before it. The rest of the town continued pelting it with objects, which it ignored as they bounced off of its scales. The mayor cut off one tentacle but another lunged forward and wrapped itself around his arm, ending on his face, cutting deep into his skin. Kinnley howled, then dropped his sword into his other arm and continued cutting into the demon's tentacles with a scream of rage.

"As we discussed!" Jodas yelled behind him.

"I know, I know!" Alys shouted, taking careful aim with her final vial from Roldin.

She let loose. The vial sailed through the air and hit home in the center of the demon-squid's chest. It let go of Kinnley and two miners rushed forward to pull him away as Jodas roared a battle cry and threw his spear at the exposed flesh where the vial had hit. The spear lodged itself deep, and the demon bellowed and shrunk back, forcing its way into the half-covered entrance of the mine to get away.

"Now, now!" the mayor screamed through the hand that covered his lacerated face.

Two more miners rushed forward with torches and lit fuses that lay nestled against the mine entrance. The town watched as the fuses slowly worked their way down the line. The demon shook its massive head, recovering from the wounds, and pulled the spear free. It bellowed at its attackers.

The fuse found its mark. The dynamite exploded, sending the townspeople diving and clamoring for cover. The entrance to the mine crumbled, vast boulders of rock from Mount Everdare coming loose and crashing down on the water with great splashes that shook the entire town. They crushed the demon that stood half-submerged in the mine opening. It was too slow to react, and rock after rock fell down upon it. They didn't see the demon die, but the sudden collapse of rock and the thin tendrils of black-tinged smoke that edged out of the cracks in the rocks and over the flood waters told them that it had worked. They cheered.

#

Roldin had gained ground on his foe, forcing the demon back, and it struggled to keep its footing on the tilted roof they were fighting on. The warrior feinted a high strike and bent low at the last moment, striking at one of the demon's legs, but his foe saw the ruse for what it was and its leg turned to mist quicker than a thought and the axe hit nothing. Roldin went off balance from the miss and made sure to roll away. Yunirax laughed and leapt back into the air and formed its wings again, taking to the skies and flying above the town. It looked around, seeing its final demon follower die at the mine, and looked back to Roldin in shock. Then it let out a terrifying screech and dove, maw first, at the demon slayer.

He met the attack with his axe held in front of him. His strike was true and it bit into exposed skin as the demon dove, but Yunirax came on anyway. It lashed out with teeth and claw and barbed sword, and caught Roldin in the side with a vicious cut. It ensnared his right wrist and squeezed. The gleaming white axe fell from his hand. Yunirax threw the demon slayer with a scream. He flew back, hitting the roof of the house next door, dazed.

"Here!" Penny called from the roof, and tossed Roldin's dark-bladed axe to him. It landed near him, but the still-stunned demon slayer shook his head and tried to focus on it. Yunirax flew over, landed on the next house and recognized Penny with a smile. The barmaid started backpedaling furiously as the demon advanced on her. Roldin recovered his wits and crawled over to the axe, lifting it with a scream, launching it through the air. The axe embedded itself in the demon's back and Yunirax let out a shriek. An impossibly long-limbed arm reached around and plucked the axe from its back, but Roldin had taken advantage of the demon's distraction and rushed forward and crashed into Yunirax with all his weight. Demon and demon slayer flew off of the roof, over a ducking Penny, and hit the plankways below with a crash.

Roldin landed on top of Yunirax and managed to wrestle his axe from its clawed hand. The overpowered demon took two mighty cuts in its chest from the axe, but the third was met with a backhanded strike across Roldin's face, knocking him back. He hit a house and shattered a window. Glass bounced on the plankway beneath him.

Both combatants stood shakily and faced one another, catching their breath. Roldin bled from a dozen small cuts on his left arm, his face, and a large gash in his side. Yunirax was winded but began repairing its damaged scales and skin as it stood. "You can't win this fight, Benirus," it said in a mocking impersonation of a woman's sultry voice.

"You've been saying that for thirty years," he growled, and rushed forward with a scream. He brought his axe around then shifted at the last minute, turning his hack into a lunge. The axe head hit bluntly into its chest and forced the demon back a step. Then Roldin brought it around with both hands and aimed low, biting into Yunirax's leg. This time the strike connected with the hard scales; the demon was tiring. He continued his dance around his foe, slashing and hacking with great speed. The demon, as large as it was, couldn't dodge quickly enough.

It struggled to change forms to compensate, shrinking in size and growing in speed as it did so. But the pain from the cuts distracted it, and as it changed forms it didn't quite do it evenly, and joints clicked awkwardly. Roldin took advantage and cut into soft flesh of a scale-less knee. The demon tripped. The demon slayer brought the axe around on its chest, striking down with screams; scales chipped and flew off in all directions. He finally found soft flesh underneath and Roldin embedded the axe deep in its chest.

Yunirax gripped the axe in its chest with one hand, then grabbed the demon slayer's head with its other. The axe was held fast. Roldin let go of it as the demon roared in wordless rage inches from his face, spittle flying from its gaping maw and causing numb spots where the drops landed on his bare skin. The demon slayer only grinned in response.

He reached down and took something from his belt, forcing the object into the demon's mouth with his left hand as it roared at him. It gagged, and Roldin brought his right hand around and punched Yunirax in the jaw. The vial of moon-iron-laced water exploded in the demon's mouth. Its eyes went wide in instant, horrific pain. Roldin reached forward, removed his axe, and struck again, cutting deeper into the demon's chest.

Even in agony, Yunirax put up a fight. It flailed its arms wildly and managed to catch the axe as Roldin brought it around for another strike, knocking the weapon into the waters below. The demon slayer screamed in frustration, then punched the hacked and vulnerable flesh where his axe had struck, again and again. He forced his hand deep into Yunirax's chest.

The demon howled at him, its mouth a ruined mess of seared flesh, and scratched at his face even as the demon slayer went wrist deep into the creature's body. He found what he was looking for and ripped the heartstone from Yunirax's gaping wound with a scream. Roldin kicked, and the demon fell into the waters below and continued to thrash in agony.

Roldin retreated along the plankway, putting distance between the heartstone and its owner. As he did so Yunirax's contorting weakened. The farther from its energy source it was the weaker the demon became.

Yunirax was barely moving now. It floated weakly in the water and stared at him with hate in its cold, red eyes. The townspeople slowly approached the scene on the plankways above, weapons still in their hands. Jodas half-carried Kinnley as they stopped and looked upon the writhing demon below them. It reached for him feebly, its claw-tipped arm futilely pawing in his direction. "You've accomplished nothing... we will find you again," it said, its feminine-like voice strained.

Roldin shook his head and said, "But I have accomplished something. I've proven that my soul, weakened as it is, still has strength. I have proven that I am something your evil kind must fear." The demon slayer raised Yunirax's heartstone in his black ash-covered, armored fist and squeezed. His arm trembled with strain. "And I have proven that I am *not* my father!"

The man squeezed with such force that the stone cracked in his grip; not much, but enough. Yunirax disappeared. Black smoke swirled above the water until it vanished completely from view.

EPILOGUE
HAPPILY EVER AFTER

Roldin shielded his eyes from the rain and searched the foggy horizon. It looked quiet and empty, other than the trees that rose out of the flood waters as if they were trying to climb out of the ocean itself. He adjusted the pack on his back and the axes on his belt, then rubbed his leg. It was healing, but not quite there yet.

He turned and was greeted by Mayor Kinnley, his arm in a sling and a jagged scar working its way down his jaw line. Even so, the portly man wore a smile. "We're going to miss you, Roldin," he said. "In our own way."

Roldin laughed. "I suppose not in too many ways."

"We'll rebuild soon enough," he said with a shrug. He looked back at the town and the work already being done to repair houses and walkways. The townspeople were jovial despite the weather and the work, mostly just happy to be alive. "We'll go on without you, slayer. Besides, now demons will think twice before coming to Road's End. We'll leave some of your traps where they are, just in case."

The demon slayer nodded. "That's the plan," he said.

The Constable appeared behind the mayor, his spear nestled formally in the crook of his arm, and handed Roldin a rolled piece of parchment.

"What's this?" the demon slayer asked.

"A pardon," Jodas said. "It won't mean much for very long, as I don't really have the authority to do that kind of thing, but as you're passing through the rest of Adren if you happen upon any guards that recognize you, you can present that to them. It has the county seal on it, so it looks genuine. Won't get you by the smarter ones, but hopefully it'll fool a couple of the idiots who wear Twill's colors."

"Thank you, very much," Roldin said. "This will help tremendously." The constable actually looked bashful. "Take care of them, Jodas."

"You know I will," he said with a quick salute.

Alys was there, too, bag on her back and, for her, only a modest amount of books packed in an overstuffed satchel on her side. "Heading back to the keep?" he asked as he extended his hand.

"What? No, silly," she said with a laugh. "I'm coming with you!"

Roldin paused. "What?"

"I've been studying the history of demons for too long," she said with a shrug. "Now I get to study their future! How can a girl pass that up? Besides," she said, hefting her pack and covering her head with a cloak, then readying a walking staff at her side, "I've read about one of the largest cult ruins ever, somewhere in the eastern mountains, its exact location lost for centuries. If we go there maybe we'll find a way to break your mark? Worth a shot, right?" As if the matter was settled, she walked over to stand next to him.

He opened his mouth to protest, then shook his head, knowing it was no use. The scholar's mind was made up.

A few of the other townspeople came to bid him

goodbye. He took hugs and well-wishes from many. The children especially crowded around him. They wore expressions of admiration on their beaming faces and yelled adulations that Roldin couldn't even begin to fathom deserving.

Finally Penny and Linder approached the crowd. They had packs on their backs, too, and behind them was a small skiff with more of their belongings inside. The demon slayer walked over to them and Penny gave him a smile. Linder lingered a few steps behind, not meeting Roldin's eyes.

"I'm sorry again," Roldin said. "This is the second time I've run you out of a town."

She raised an eyebrow and feigned an angry face at him. "I know it's the best way to keep the town and us safe," she said with a shrug. "I was getting tired of tending bar anyway, and made a nice bit of coin selling my half to Wull. Besides, I've always wanted to see—"

"Nope," he said with a grin, quickly putting a finger to her lips that he promptly drew back awkwardly. "I can't know where you're going. That defeats the whole point."

"I know, I know," she said. Penny looked back and giggled softly at Linder's forlorn expression as the boy kicked at the plankways at his feet. "He's never liked goodbyes," she explained with a sad smile. Penny took a deep breath and looked Roldin in the eye. "Never thought I'd say this to the no-good phony Krill Tempest, but I'm going to miss you."

"I'll miss you, too," the demon slayer said, and she came forward to hug him. As they released she planted a quick kiss on his cheek.

Roldin bent down, with only a little discomfort from his leg, and tried to meet Linder's eyes. "Linder," he said.

"Linder. I have something for you."

This got the child's attention. He walked over slowly as Roldin took out a book from his pack and handed it to him. The boy read the title out loud: "*The Pauper Prince and the Sword of Kuralee.*"

"This," Roldin said, putting his hand on the book, "was my most favorite story when I was your age. It taught me many things, including the kind of person I wanted to be when I grew up. A good friend let me give it to you," he said, smiling briefly at Alys. "I want you to read it and whenever you do, remember that somewhere out there, I'm thinking of you, too."

The boy smiled excitedly, hefting the huge tome in his hands. Abruptly his face grew grave, and he looked at Roldin uncertainly. "But...how does it end?" he asked.

The demon slayer leaned in close and whispered, "They lived happily ever after."

Linder rushed forward and hugged Roldin fiercely.

"Despite all this," Roldin addressed Penny and Linder as he stood, "I think I'll be seeing you both again."

"Why do you say that?" the former barmaid asked with a sly grin.

"I'll have to find you to get my dagger back," he said with a glint in his eye. Penny touched her hand to the ornate dagger at her belt. "I still have one more use for it."

With that, Roldin Benirus straightened his pack, wiggled his toes in his boots, and raised his hand to the people of Road's End. The crowd cheered as he and Alys walked down the plankways, and immediately halved their progress by wading through the flood waters of the forest below Mount Everdare. The crowd behind him kept waving, though, a little awkwardly, as the minutes dragged on and the two were still well in sight.

That didn't stop Roldin from turning one last time, seeing Penny and Linder still watching him, and giving them one last wave.

"This is so exciting!" Alys exclaimed. "Here we are, adventuring! Traveling—though slowly! Wading through muck just like in the tales—though, the tales were never this smelly."

Roldin didn't say anything. They kept shuffling through the flood waters and eventually reached drier land. They took refuge from the rain under a tree and drained their boots of water and mud.

"So, now, where to?" Alys asked.

"Your mountain sounds good enough," he replied.

"Let's go!" she said bouncily and hopped on ahead. She had to stop and wait for Roldin to put his boots back on and rub his sore leg for a moment. He let out a good cough.

The demon slayer finally joined her on the path. "I bet you've never traveled with another person before, huh?" Alys asked with a grin.

Roldin shrugged. He put a hand to the gleaming white axe that hung at his right side. It was warm to the touch, even in the pouring rain and the chilly morning air. He closed his eyes and thought of his friend. "I guess some things do change," he mused quietly.

The rain stopped. Roldin looked up and saw the smallest patch of blue sky show itself through the swirling grey clouds.

He smiled.

ABOUT THE AUTHOR

The author is a daydreamer who accidentally grew up.
He was raised in the southern United States to a loving
mother and father who would never sell his soul to
demons. He lives in the northeast with a girl silly enough
to marry him and enjoys playing games, dreaming of
other worlds, and writing things.

Ransom Prestridge is one of you.

THIS BOOK WOULD NOT HAVE BEEN POSSIBLE WITHOUT

Liz,
and her gift of finding the diamonds in the rough drafts

Kevin,
and his gift of hearing through my rambling and believing in the story

Sylvia,
and her gift of seeing what my mind's palette saw before I did

My wife,
and her gift of patience and love as I chased a dream

My father,
and his giving me life and encouraging me to follow my passions

Authors everywhere,
for their gift of lighting the fire of my imagination